AN ANTHOLOGY OF
RURAL STORIES BY WRITERS
OF COLOR, 2025

AN ANTHOLOGY
OF RURAL
STORIES BY
WRITERS OF
COLOR, 2025

ISBN: 978-1-958094-67-9

EastOver Press encourages the use of our publications
in educational settings. For questions about
educational discounts, contact us online:
www.EastOverPress.com or info@EastOverPress.com.

Book Design by Beste M. Doğan

10 9 8 7 6 5 4 3 2 1

Published in the United States of America by

EASTOVER PRESS
Rochester, Massachusetts
www.EastOverPress.com

EastOver
PRESS

---

an

ANTHOLOGY

of

RURAL

STORIES

by

WRITERS

of

COLOR,

2025

---

edited by

Deesha
Philyaw

TABLE OF CONTENTS

FOREWORD

Creating and sustaining this anthology of rural stories by writers of color, now in its third iteration, has truly been one of the greatest pleasures of my writing life. There's an indescribable joy in connecting with other short story writers, many of whom I've not met in person but still feel a special kinship. There's a connection, I think, with not only the form but with the brave work of putting words on the page. A small show of protest. An exercise in pure democracy. An acknowledgment of faith in our communities, literary and otherwise.

I, myself, mostly write short stories. Sure, I've penned a few poems, and I've certainly tried my hand—like most fiction writers I know—at a longer form (shall we call it a novel?). But for me nothing has the call back power of a short story. It's what I naturally gravitate toward when perusing online journals or browsing shelves at an indie or used book store. Simply put: I love the short story. It's what I love to read and write.

It's for all these reasons that I love this anthology. We receive dozens of submissions, from both editors and authors alike, and we at EastOver Press select around forty to send to a guest editor. This year, our guest editor was the incomparable Deesha Philyaw, author of the esteemed *The Secret Lives of Church Ladies*. We asked Deesha to select around 15 stories for the anthology (she chose 16), and each of the stories in its own way was a pure delight: in two cases we're featuring stories of first publication. "Uncle Tito" by Noah Alvarez was first published, as the author's first publication, in *Cutleaf Journal*. In another case, we're publishing a story that hasn't been previously published. What you'll read here is C.G. Crawford's first published story. In other cases, you'll read excellent work from well-established short story writers whose work has been published in some of the finest literary journals in the country.

It feels important to me to mention that I am also the fiction editor at *Cutleaf Journal*, and I nominated several stories for consideration, with no expectation that Deesha would choose any of them. She ended up choosing three. Upon learning this, I felt both excited (we at *Cutleaf* are publishing work that other writers like!) and sheepish (three out of the sixteen stories belong to one journal where I am fiction editor). There's no more to say about it, but I felt it necessary to at least acknowledge this fact. Of course it goes without saying that the other thirteen stories included are pure delights in their own way.

Lastly, I'd like to acknowledge that in almost every one of these introductions or forewords to anthologies featuring short stories there exists in some form the predictable and maybe, now, obligatory defense of the short story. Or maybe an assurance that the short story is alive and well. Originally, I wanted to say that I felt no need to defend, stick up for, or otherwise assure readers of this notion. Partly, I suppose, because it matters very little to me if people read short stories. What matters to me most is that short stories find readers who care as much about short stories as I do, such as you, Reader, holding this anthology. And I will add my own affirmation here, based on the stories herein: the short story *is* alive and well. And, from my vantage point, thriving—living its fullest and best life as the preeminent fictional form. Let it be known.

Keith Pilapil Lesmeister, 2025

INTRODUCTION

Before reading the submissions for this anthology, I thought about what shape it might take, what kinds of stories I hoped to feature. I wanted stories that reflected an expansive view of "rural." I also wanted weirdness, for sure. Experimental narratives. Transgressive, risk-taking tales. And I hoped there would be some stories about race that surprised me, maybe even made me laugh. I'm happy to report that the stories I ultimately selected, gathered here, are all this and more, in beautiful and unexpected ways.

With confident prose, these rural stories cover a wide berth:

a Tampa trailer park and the "blacktopped guts of Florida," farms, the 'hood, a shotgun house in West Alabama, small-town Missouri, cadavers on three and a half acres of grasslands, the silver mirror lakes and serpentine roads of Tahoe, an Osage Indian reservation, a mansion on the "forested edge of New Jersey," a night train from Bangalore to Madras, India. The Confederate flag makes an appearance. Across these landscapes and the 20th and 21st centuries, we meet characters, some of whom are grappling with spoken and unspoken desires, loss, and grief. Others dare to upend social and cultural expectations. One young narrator longs for "a life gentle enough to accommodate the smaller aches"; in this way, she is like many of the freshly drawn characters you'll meet in this collection.

In half of the stories, a house or home is central; these stories elucidate the difference between the two. Here, houses are sites of comfort and memory, but also duplicity, betrayal, sadness, and denial. Some houses are unsafe, others are sanctuaries.

Mothers, who can be a kind of home, are also present in significant numbers here. A Mississippi mama who would not love. Mamas missing due to death or divorce or because she just dipped. Screaming, disillusioned, hard-working mothers. And one Mexican mother who exacts the sweetest revenge.

I'm grateful to the writers represented here; their stories inspired me to do two of my favorite things: write and research. As I read, I jotted notes for a new story?/novella?/novel? -in-progress of my own that has a strong sense of place. *How do I immerse the reader in the physical and psychological spaces of the narrative in the first sentence or paragraph? How do I make my characters reflect the places they're from or trying to escape from—without caricaturing them? How do I seamlessly include artistic, geographic, and scientific details to give the story depth and texture? How do I write about race in ways that decenter whiteness while at the same time confronting it? These are all things the stories in this anthology do so well.*

After reading these stories late into the night, I would often fall down Google search rabbit holes: "Anasazi pottery bowl," "beer and butter sauce ingredients," "Can sixteen-year-olds work as mail carriers?" and more. I searched partly because I'm a nerd and a Virgo, but mostly because I simply did not want to leave the worlds these characters inhabited.

My wish for you, fellow readers, is that these stories will also pique your curiosity, challenge your convictions, inform your creativity, and entertain you, long after the last page.

Deesha Philyaw, 2025

an
ANTHOLOGY
of
RURAL
STORIES
by
WRITERS
of
COLOR,
2025

UNCLE TITO

by
NOAH ALVAREZ
Published in *Cutleaf*

Uncle Tito had been living with us for the past two months. I thought it was the coolest thing in the world having him at the house. But Mom and Jerry didn't want him to move in at first. They said it would be like taking care of another kid because of how sick he was. He had lost his house, his car, and his pride. So Mom gave in.

In October, I made the freshman basketball team. On the night of our first game, I rode to the gym in the backseat of the Volvo. Jerry drove and Uncle Tito sat shotgun. On the way to the game, Jerry had to drop Uncle Tito off at the Y for a meeting. If

Uncle Tito missed one meeting he was done. It was Jerry's rule.

Uncle Tito wore a wife-beater under his cigarette-scented flannel and a gold Jesus-piece around his neck. He carried a plastic water cup in his hand. He could never keep his hands still. He wore his sunglasses everywhere, even at night and indoors.

Uncle Tito drummed his fingers on his thighs. He was self-conscious of people looking at his hands when they shook, so he always kept them moving. Jerry leaned forward over the steering wheel and tried to ignore him.

Why are you so jumpy over there, Tito, said Jerry. You didn't mistake the Grey Goose for water did you?

Very funny, Jerry, said Uncle Tito.

Uncle Tito smiled and tried to brush it off, but he'd been working hard to try and stay sober, and Jerry knew how to get under his skin.

Uncle Tito looked at me in the rearview.

You excited for your first game, squirt?

He doesn't like it when you call him that, said Jerry.

He doesn't like it when you call him that, mocked Uncle Tito. I tried not to laugh but I couldn't help it. Uncle Tito smiled and Jerry looked back at me disapproving.

I've known the boy longer than you have, said Uncle Tito. I've been watching him play since he started back in the third grade. I can name every team he's played for. I can't even remember the last time I saw you at a game, Jerry.

I forget that you don't know what it's like to have a job, said Jerry. Or responsibilities.

I'm excited, I said. I wish one of you guys could come watch.

I know, buddy, said Jerry. I'd be at every game if I didn't have to work. Your mother is proud.

I don't think he likes being called buddy, said Uncle Tito.

Jerry tightened his grip on the steering wheel. We pulled up to the curb in front of the Y.

This is your stop, said Jerry. Don't stumble in there now.

Uncle Tito ignored Jerry. He unbuckled his seatbelt and turned to me. He lowered his glasses and looked at me with his yellow-tinted eyes.

Lights out tonight, kid, he said.

Uncle Tito winked and jumped out of the car. He closed the door and I climbed to the front. He waved at us as we drove by. I waved back and Jerry floored the gas.

Prick, Jerry mumbled.

I think it's awesome having Uncle Tito around, I said. He's been doing really good with us.

Don't expect it to last, said Jerry.

$$\bullet \ \bullet \ \bullet$$

I got home from school the next day and Uncle Tito had moved the futon from against the wall to right in front of the TV. Our house only had two bedrooms and one bath. The living room had become his room and the futon had become his bed.

Uncle Tito was smoking a cigarette and taking big gulps of his water. He was watching a Celtics game that he had recorded the night before. He never watched basketball for pleasure. He was constantly studying each game with unbreakable focus.

I was on the way to my room when he called for me.

Hey, big head! Come sit down. I want to show you something from this game.

I went in the living room and sat down next to him. The smoke was unbearable and he kept taking drags.

You can learn so much from these guys, he said.

Uncle Tito had gone to the same high school I went to, and back in the eighties he was the star point guard. He was only five-foot-ten and a hundred and fifty pounds, but he led the state in scoring, assists and steals three years in a row. He was named the state's Mr. Basketball his senior year.

He was on his way to a full ride to Fresno State before he tore his ACL in the state semi's his senior year. After the injury, he lost all the speed and agility that made him a star, and Fresno State lost interest. He played half a year of ball for a junior college in Illinois but he had to drop out because he flunked all of his classes.

Uncle Tito put his arm around me and pointed to the screen.

You're a good shooter, kid, but you're letting too many opportunities slip away because you're not attacking the basket. Look here.

He paused the game.

Look at the ball-handler here. He doesn't do anything special. Just a quick one-two dribble to get his defender off balance. Then he drives to the basket. Easy lay-up.

You haven't been to any of my games this year, I said.

But I've watched every single one. They come on public access. If I'm at a meeting, I record them and watch them after. Look.

Uncle Tito switched to a recording of my last game and we watched the first few minutes.

Man, he said. When you dribble up the court, your hair bounces on your head just like mine did.

I was about to ask him something when Mom stormed in the house. Uncle Tito tried to ash the cigarette before she came in the living room. She stood in the doorway with her hands on her hips.

Goddamnit Tito! she yelled. I told you a million times *not* in the house! Jerry is looking for any reason to throw your stupid ass out. And in front of your nephew?

She came and snatched the cigarette from his hand. I don't understand why you always have to act like a jackass, she said.

Mom turned to me and cocked her head.

To your room, now, she said. You have homework. And you, she turned to Uncle Tito. Get your lazy ass up and help with the groceries.

We both stood up, a little ashamed, and followed our orders.

Before I went to my room, Uncle Tito patted me on the back.

We'll watch it after dinner tonight, he said.

I closed the door to my room, too excited to start my homework.

• • •

One night Uncle Tito's meeting got cancelled. That same night we had a game against our rivals, Alderson Catholic. Mom agreed to take Uncle Tito to the game with me since she had a babysitting gig and couldn't stay to watch.

In the car Uncle Tito didn't shake as much. He rubbed his hands together and said things like, It's going to be a good one tonight. He acted like he was going to suit up himself.

Do you have your water cup? Mom asked Uncle Tito.

Yes.

I'm just making sure. And you know the school is a smoke free zone, right? No smoking outside the gym door.

It's a two-hour game. You don't think I can make it two hours without smoking?

I'm just reminding you, Tito.

Mom pulled up to the gym entrance.

I'll be back around nine-thirty to pick you guys up, she said. She rubbed her hand on my knee. Good luck, honey.

The boy doesn't need luck, said Uncle Tito.

We walked to the big glass doors. Uncle Tito was behind me rubbing my shoulders. When we went through the doors into the foyer Uncle Tito looked up at the high ceiling. The lights were bright and he looked out of place in his old school.

It feels different, he said. He stood in the middle of the foyer.

The gym is this way, Uncle Tito.

He continued behind me but kept looking around, up at the ceiling and over his shoulder.

On the wall just before the gym doors was *The Wall of Excellence*. It was a glass-display of the school's best sports teams and athletes over the years. There were pictures of the old football team before it was disbanded in ninety-four, and there were pictures of the current state quarterfinalist in tennis, Sarah Hash. But no section was as coveted as the basketball area.

Our school had never won a championship in anything, but the basketball team was the closest we ever came. Uncle Tito stopped in front of the display and pulled his sunglasses down. An official game ball sat in a case with two jerseys hung above it on either side, one white and one navy blue. Both had the number *6*.

My fucking jerseys, said Uncle Tito. He sounded surprised and upset at the same time.

It's the only number no one is allowed to wear, I said.

Uncle Tito looked around the display case and spotted a wooden plaque with gold lettering. Above the words was a picture of a young man with sharp cheekbones and curly hair who posed like a soldier in his jersey. Uncle Tito nearly dropped his water cup.

*This plaque is a symbol of recognition to Tatum "Tito"
Petrola School and State leader in points, assists and steals
Tatum is a first team all-state selection, as well as an
academic all-state member*

I watched him study the picture and the words under it. I felt proud to be standing next to him and his plaque. My friends loved to remind me that was my uncle in the picture. But Uncle Tito didn't even smirk at it. He threw his sunglasses back on his face and continued to the gym.

They need to take that shit down, he said. My records were broken seven years ago.

• • •

After the game, we sat on the curb outside and waited for Mom to pick us up. Uncle Tito was trying to think of something encouraging to say.

It is what it is, kid, he said.

We lost by thirty-four, I said pitifully.

Yea. The team sucked tonight. But you had twenty points tonight, so *you* didn't suck, right? Man, I swear you're getting better.

I was past the point of frustration. I was tired and the sweat on my body had dried and made me cold.

Behind us the doors flew open. The three referees who called our game came out, all of them talking. Two of them went to the right towards the parking lot. The third, a tall, skinny guy, walked towards us. He was parked in the student parking lot on the other side. As he passed us him and Uncle Tito made eye contact. He stopped and a smile spread across his face.

Son of a bitch, he said. It's Tito Petrola! You're Tito Petrola! He put his hands on his head in disbelief. I knew that was you up in the bleachers man!

Do I know you? said Uncle Tito.

I played for Hillsborough back in the day man. I was, like, a sophomore when you were a senior. You dropped forty points on us in the playoffs! No one could guard you man!

Oh yea, I remember that.

I can't believe you're sitting in front of me. Everyone used to talk about you. You're the best player this state's ever seen. Man!

Uncle Tito folded his hands to keep them from shaking. He didn't look all the way up at the man.

Then the man pointed at me, like he hadn't noticed me the whole time.

Wow, and now your son's out here playing ball too, he said.

I waited for Uncle Tito to correct him but he didn't. Instead, he just smirked.

Tito, your boy's a spitting image of you. He turned to me and pointed to Tito. Hey kid, when your old man was your age, no one he played against could stop him. Every shot he put up found the net.

The man felt around for his keys in his pocket and turned his truck on with them. He drove a new, white Ford and he started to walk backwards towards it.

Tito fucking Petrola, he said. Man. Make sure you come to the next game and say what's up.

He turned around and kept walking.

Tito Petrola, I heard him say again. Then he got in his truck and pulled off.

Uncle Tito didn't speak. We sat there like the encounter hadn't happened. He tried to clear the phlegm from his throat but couldn't. Then he lowered his head and threw up between his legs. It was mostly bile mixed with a few chunks of the pasta we'd had for dinner. I stood up and backed away.

I'm fine, he said. He waved his hand in the air to confirm it. I just need a damn cigarette. Where the hell is your mom?

A few minutes later the Volvo pulled up. It was too dark for Mom to see the vomit on the ground.

Don't tell her a damn thing, said Uncle Tito before we opened the doors. He got in the back seat.

You're taking the back, Tito? said Mom.

The boy played hard. He deserves it. But he doesn't want to talk about it.

Tough night, huh? she asked me.

I said he doesn't want to talk about it.

All right, all right, damn, said Mom. Are you feeling ok, Tito?

Tito didn't respond. He was upset but I couldn't tell if it was about basketball or that guy bugging him, or if maybe he was actually sick. But I didn't think about it too much. He would feel better tomorrow.

• • •

Uncle Tito didn't let me mope around after the game. He told me to quit being soft and put in the extra work to make sure a game like that never happened again. Every day we didn't have practice I was putting up shots in the backyard. Uncle Tito would smoke and watch me.

Shoulders squared, he would say over and over. Elbow in. Come on now.

One day I struggled with my shot and Uncle Tito yelled these things over and over. I put the ball down and held my hands on top of my head to breathe.

You're exhausted, he said. That's why you're not shooting consistently.

Hey Uncle, Tito, how come you never shoot hoops anymore?

Uncle Tito crossed his arms and thought about it.

Well, he said, I just don't anymore, I guess. I don't know. I'd probably throw my back out if I tried.

I picked up the ball and held it towards him.

I bet you still got it.

Not anymore, kid. Haven't touched a ball in years.

Come on, Uncle Tito. How are you going to coach me if you can't lead by example?

Don't get smart, kid.

Just a shot or two and I'll leave you alone. Deal?

Uncle Tito hesitated but he finally took a deep breath and stood. He popped his neck to the left and right and clapped for the ball. I passed it to him. He came to where I was and put the ball down to stretch his arms across his chest and both of his shoulders popped. He picked the ball back up and spun it on the tip of his middle finger and let it spin like it was a muscle on his body he was flexing. Then he tossed it from his finger and caught it in his hands and put his forehead to it as if in prayer.

Prepare to be disappointed, he said.

His beer gut hung from the bottom of his shirt and his shoulders were slumped forward. He moved like he was thirty years older than he was. He barely bent his knees and his feet barely left the ground but the shot he put up was graceful when it left his fingertips. His elbow extended smoothly and the flick of his wrist was like a cherry on a sundae.

The ball spiraled high in the air and dropped through the hoop and splashed against the net like water. The rim did not rattle.

Well, he said, I guess I still got it. Let me see it again.

I passed him the ball and he put up another shot. Nothing but net. I kept grabbing his rebounds for him and he kept putting them up. Out of forty shots he only missed two. I noticed Mom watching us from the kitchen window. Normally at this time in the evening she'd call us in for chores or dinner. But tonight she just smiled and let us play.

Me and Uncle Tito started a game of H.O.R.S.E. but we only got to O before it was too dark to see the ball. I kicked my shoes off on the patio and looked over at Uncle Tito. I hadn't realized how exhausted he was from putting up all those shots. He struggled to get each breath out of his throat. He was bent down with his hands on his knees. I took his arm and put it around my back and helped him into the house onto the futon.

Jerry was on the recliner reading something on his phone.

Jesus Christ, he said, flaring his nostrils. Would it kill you to hop in the shower real quick before dinner?

Suck a fat one, Jerry.

Will you two shut up? Mom yelled from the kitchen. I'm not dealing with your all's bullshit tonight.

Jerry stood up and walked to the kitchen. He mumbled something under his breath before he was out of the room. Uncle Tito was still panting on the futon and didn't notice. Or he was too tired to respond.

• • •

After dinner, I lay in my room and skimmed through a book I had to read for a book report. It was eleven at night and I was already supposed to be asleep but I kept hearing what sounded like a cat pushing out a hairball. I put the book down and creeped over to the door and cracked it open. I realized it was Uncle Tito dry heaving.

Just lay down, I heard Mom say in a weak voice. Uncle Tito moaned and the springs in the futon squeaked under his weight.

It was just a game of H.O.R.S.E, said Uncle Tito. Is that all it's going to take to kill me?

It's just a headache, said Mom. You're exercising again and you're tired. That's a good thing. That can be your success story for your meeting tomorrow.

Mom started to hum something. She got quieter and quieter and then stopped. He must have fallen asleep. I heard her walk to her room. Before she opened her door I could hear her sniffle. I thought she was going to cry. She went in her room and quietly shut the door.

• • •

When the weather got cold everyone's mood got worse. Jerry started working six days a week and Uncle Tito started going to the doctor, which meant Mom had to drop her baby-sitting gig to keep up with his appointments and meetings.

One day I found blood in the toilet. When I asked Mom about it she didn't say who it was. But Uncle Tito's skin was turning yellow and he couldn't keep his food down, so I put two and two together.

Uncle Tito and Jerry didn't go back and forth like they used to. Instead Mom would give Jerry that mean look to make him do something that showed he at least pretended to care about Uncle Tito. He would refill his water cup or get him a dinner plate or a barf bag. Uncle Tito didn't even crack jokes. They weren't cordial but they dealt with each other, like there was some cold understanding between them.

He stopped wearing his sunglasses and he only got up from the futon to go to the bathroom. He kept a plastic bag with him just in case he got the spins. He only watched *Wheel of Fortune* and other boring game shows on TV but he never actually paid attention to what was going on. It was like Uncle Tito was never actually there anymore. He even stopped talking to me about basketball.

One night I sat next to him while he was watching *Wheel of Fortune*. His skin smelled rotted and he looked lost staring at the TV.

Is there any way you could come to our game tomorrow night? I asked. If we win, we make the freshman team playoffs.

I have to go to the doctor's office tomorrow, he said. He didn't bother to turn from the TV to answer.

Oh.

If you haven't noticed, I can't really go anywhere anymore.

I just thought that maybe—

Let me shoot it straight with you, kid, he said. He bent over to look in the kitchen. Mom had her headphones in while she cooked.

It's time for you to understand what's going on. I'm going to need a new liver if I ever want to be normal again.

But I thought you stopped drinking?

I did. I've been sober for eight months now. The thing is, the damage has already been done. I went twenty-six years drinking every single day and I didn't stop soon enough to save myself. I'm lucky I bought myself a few extra months by quitting when I did.

I sat there with my mouth open trying to think of something to say.

Just don't make a big deal about it, he said. It's my own fault.

Dinner's ready! Mom called from the kitchen.

I'll make you a plate, I said to Uncle Tito. He patted my shoulder.

You're a good kid, he said. Sometimes I wish you were my own.

I went in the kitchen and got him a small bowl of chili. I handed it to him and went for mine.

Why are you moping around? Mom asked.

I didn't answer. I took my chili to my room and let it go cold on my dresser.

• • •

The next night was the biggest game of my life but I had no motivation to play. I walked home from the bus stop and dreaded putting on my jersey or shooting a ball or seeing Uncle Tito. I resented him for not being able to come to the game.

I got home and took a nap and then ate dinner. At six-thirty I got my gear together and went out to the car. Mom sat behind the wheel with the engine running. I didn't notice Uncle Tito was sitting in the back until I got in the passenger seat.

I was surprised to see him. He had on one of his navy blue high school jerseys over his hoodie and his sunglasses. He smiled at me when I got in the car. It was the happiest I had seen him in weeks. There were a hundred things I wanted to ask him about from the day before but none of them were worth mentioning now, as if those problems just didn't exist anymore.

You're letting me sit up front? I said.

Why not? Special treatment for the star player, right?

Mom took off and Uncle Tito put his hands on my shoulders and squeezed.

I thought you said you weren't watching the game, I said.

It's the biggest game of the year. Just cause I can't be there in person doesn't mean I'm not watching.

I had spent the whole night prior making myself understand that Uncle Tito was too sick to focus on basketball right now, which made me hate the thought of basketball. Now that I knew he was watching tonight's game I was ecstatic. And then I felt the pressure to win. I started to tense up in the front seat.

We pulled into the school parking lot. Uncle Tito reached behind his neck and unhooked his Jesus-piece. He held it delicately in the air and looked at it for a moment. Then he handed it to me.

I guess it's time I hand it down to its heir, he said.

I stared at it and watched it glisten. He kept dangling it.

Take it before I change my mind, he said.

I took it and hooked it around my neck.

It was your grandad's. He gave it to me before he passed away my senior year. It used to be my good luck charm.

I ran my fingers down the gold chain. I couldn't believe I was actually wearing it.

He looks just like you, Mom said.

Before I got too carried away Uncle Tito gave me a noogie.

You're going to be late, dummy, he said. He lightly pushed me towards the door and I got out. Uncle Tito got out and went around to the front.

Remember, channel four, I said.

I know what channel smart ass, he said. He got in and Mom blew me a kiss and they drove away. I fingered the cross on my chest the whole way inside.

• • •

The gym was so empty that it would have made the game feel less significant any other night. That's how freshman games were. There were maybe three pairs of parents in the stands and a group of pot-heads sitting in the far corner. But it felt like the whole world was watching me from home. I could see Uncle Tito leaning forward on the futon blowing into his fists, Mom begging him to lean back and relax.

The boys on Denton Valley were as big as trees. Their arms

were the size of my head and any of them could have passed for seniors. The whistle blew and our center didn't bother jumping for the tip. We immediately retreated to defense.

Their center was a fourteen-year-old who was six-foot-seven. As soon as he touched the ball he bullied our center in the post, backed him in and put up an easy layup. He put up ten straight points just like that before we could get one of our own.

I was trying to get my teammates involved the first quarter but every shot they put up clanked off the side of the rim. They made a few bad passes that went out of bounds and Denton Valley's point guard got a couple of steals and that's how the first quarter ended. I walked to the bench ahead of my teammates and pouted.

I heard Uncle Tito in my head. Quit acting like that, he said. If you don't want to lose, then take control of the game.

I gave my teammates fists bumps on the bench and tried to act optimistic about the second quarter. Our big man set some screens for me and I hit a couple of threes. We stole the ball a few times for some fast-break layups. But we didn't have anyone big enough to stop their lumberjacks in the post. They put up points effortlessly. Before the halftime buzzer sounded their center caught an inbound pass and dunked the ball with both hands and made the frame of the backboard rattle. I had scored fifteen points so far and felt better until I looked up at the scoreboard. We only had fifteen points to their thirty-one.

We sat in the locker room at halftime with our heads down

like the game was already lost. Our coach let us sit in silence and stared at us, disappointed. He shook his head and told us how sorry we were.

I could see Uncle Tito pacing around the living room cussing at the TV, calling us soft and pitiful. Our coach wasn't going to say anything useful and Uncle Tito expected me to do something. So I took control of the room.

What the hell's gotten into us? I yelled. I looked at my teammates with my fists clenched. My voice echoed around the locker room.

Why are we scared to shoot the fucking ball? It doesn't matter how big they are. They're too fat and slow to keep up with us. We should be running circles around them!

My teammates sat wide-eyed and some of them straightened up. Some of them nodded their heads at what I was saying.

We can't be scared to lose. If we play scared to lose we'll miss out on every opportunity we have to win. If they hit us, that's fine. We'll take the foul shots. I'll even score every fucking point if I have to. But I need all of you to give me everything you've got. Do you understand?

My teammates didn't say anything but I felt a spark in the room. They stood up and circled around me. I could feel the urgency to win. I fingered the cross on my chest and put my hand up to break it down.

Family on three! I yelled. One. Two. Three!

• • •

We came out like a different team in the third quarter. I hit three straight threes and my teammates knocked down a few more. Finally, Denton Valley was getting tired and they started to miss. We took advantage of every rebound and scored on fast-breaks. We cut their lead down to six with three minutes to go in the third.

On defense I lost my man on a screen and I got stuck guarding big boy. He could have picked me up and tossed me across the court like a tennis ball if he wanted to. He pushed me back with his shoulder and demanded the ball down low.

He got the ball and dribbled a couple of times. I tried to go for it but my arms couldn't reach around his waist. He put his head down again and pushed me off-balance. Then he pushed again to get to his spot under the basket, but instead of trying to push back I stepped to the side and let gravity take care of him. Without the resistance he expected, he fell forward with all of his weight. There was a loud *thump* on the hardwood and he lay there with his hands over his face. I could see Uncle Tito standing in the living room with his arms crossed, nodding his head. He had told me the most important thing you can do is play smarter, not harder.

The big man was sent to the locker room with a concussion and all of Denton Valley's momentum left with him. The fourth quarter came around and by then it was a different game. I hit another four three pointers and my teammates kept coming up with steals that led to easy buckets. Denton Valley was exhausted and we were playing like the game had just started. We outscored them twenty-four to zero in the fourth quarter. The clock ticked down and when the buzzer sounded I looked up at the scoreboard.

Fifty-five to forty. We were in the playoffs.

• • •

We celebrated on the sideline, giving each other hugs and chanting *Playoffs* before the ref made us line up to shake hands with Denton Valley. They looked angry and on the verge of tears when we passed them. Afterwards, I looked to my right and saw Jerry standing on the court, away from the other parents. I walked up to him, and even though he wasn't smiling I was excited to see him.

What are you doing here? I asked him.

I'm here to pick you up.

Did you watch the game? We're going to the playoffs!

I haven't been here for long. We need to go to the car.

I'm supposed to go to the locker room first. We always meet in the locker room after the game.

We don't have time, kid. Get your bag and let's go.

He sounded frustrated and I was anxious following him to the parking lot. He didn't look at me or anyone else when we walked outside. He kept his head down and we got in the car.

What's the matter? I said. Where are we going?

We have to get to the hospital, he said. He sped out of the parking lot and ran a red light as we left the neighborhood.

Are Mom and Uncle Tito there?

Yes.

Is Uncle Tito alright?

Jerry thought about it. His hesitation told me everything I needed to know. He kept his eyes on the road and sighed.

I don't think so, buddy.

I looked out the window and didn't ask anything else. I didn't care about Jerry or the game we won or my new necklace. Even though the buildings and people were blurs as we drove by and we ran stop signs and another red light, it didn't feel like we were going fast enough.

THE KITCHEN

by
VICTORIA BALLESTEROS
Published in *Cutleaf*

The small, narrow kitchen at 12257 Behrens Avenue was the busiest on the street, maybe the whole neighborhood. In addition to my eight older siblings and I constantly searching for something to eat, our home featured a reliable stream of hungry kids from the neighborhood availing themselves of my mamá's cooking. These transients would straggle in just as the sun was setting and *Three's Company* was coming on the TV. Mamá had a "Mi Casa es Su Casa" tile hanging above the dining table, and by all appearances, she meant it.

Shawn, with her short blonde hair and Vidal Sassoon jeans, would come from the southeast corner of the street, while Courtney in her pale blue ditto bell bottoms descended from the dead-end corner to the north. They would show up at least a few days a week in search of Mamá's tacos.

Gabriel and his little sister Maria would simply walk over from next door. Maria had been born with one hairy brown werewolf arm that was longer than the other, and problematic in that I couldn't stop staring at it when she was around, causing me to lose my appetite. I would slide my plate over and watch as she and her brother devoured my enchiladas without saying a word. It was an effective strategy on their part.

Sidney Wade from three houses down would also show up for a seat at the table. The Wades were transplants from Oklahoma. The family was about as big as ours, and poorer. Their house was always alive with hillbilly drama that would end with little Sidney getting whipped by his mama with a switch off the willow tree. Come dinnertime, he'd be standing barefoot in our kitchen, his tattered overalls several inches too short, avoiding eye contact with Mamá as she handed him a plate. We imagined that his family survived on a diet of acorns and squirrels, so we felt sorry for him and pretended not to see when he'd stuff tortillas in his pockets before leaving.

My siblings and I didn't care about random kids from the 'hood eating our food. We were tired of beans and tortillas and didn't see the novelty in Mamá's culinary offerings the way they did. Besides, on occasion we were lucky enough to be at their houses when their moms made things like Top Ramen noodles - an elusive delicacy - or Hungry-Man dinners from the oven, which didn't taste so great but at least it wasn't beans. My brothers would sometimes head to Durrell and Keisha's house to swap pan dulce for cornbread and greens. In my opinion, bologna sandwiches with Fritos and cherry Kool-Aid from Patty's mom were the best.

The kitchen was my favorite place in the house because that's where Mamá could be found. She always said a woman's job is to take care of everyone else, so she spent her days cooking and cleaning and looking after the kids and the husband and the nonstop visitors. Mamá kept a chair next to the sink for me to stand on when I washed the dishes, to help me reach the faucet. When I wanted one-on-one time with her, I would sit in that chair and watch as she maneuvered a massive ear of cactus, careful not to stick herself with the thorns, or peeled a boiled cow tongue, sorted beans, or rolled tamales in corn husks for the Christmas feast. When I had a stomachache in the middle of the night my poor tired mamá would bring me to the kitchen, heat water in a saucepan, and add dried manzanilla or yerba buena from the garden for a tea that would soothe both my belly and my spirits. If I had nightmares about flying snakes and spiders, Mamá would sit me down and give me something sweet to chase away the fear.

The kitchen had a window just above the sink with a view of the giant ficus tree in our front yard, which overlooked the northbound 605 freeway. Sometimes Mamá would stand at the sink sorting and washing the beans, her gaze fixed on the horizon. Papá never let her learn how to drive, so she would spend hours watching the cars go by. Once, I asked her what she was doing.

"I'm counting the red cars, mija," she said.

Later, I asked her again.

"I'm counting blue cars, mija," she said.

And again, I asked her.

"I'm counting brown cars."

Some days she would do this until the sun started to set, its orange light peeking through the sheer white curtains, illuminating the brown linoleum floor with golden specks. That was her cue to get back to serving everyone dinner.

Across from the sink was the refrigerator, a white 1960s electrocution hazard. The refrigerator was split, with a metal icebox up on top that would grow two inches of frost all around the inside perimeter. Mamá would defrost it using a butter knife to chop her way through the thick ice, putting herself in the hands of the Virgen de Guadalupe to protect her from electrical shock. On the bottom was the cooler with a door that must've weighed 100 pounds. That didn't stop my siblings and I from opening it several dozen times a day, thinking somehow the contents of Coors and beans had changed in the few minutes since we last peeked inside. We took a gamble each time we pulled open that door, as we would sometimes get zapped by the steel handle.

Will I get electrocuted this time?

Nope.

What about this time?

Nope.

This time?

BZZZZZT!

A vibration of current would shoot from my hand, up my arm to my shoulders, and to the top of my head as my legs wobbled like peach Jello.

On the weekends I would come home from my religious classes to fetch beers out of the fridge for my papá and his brothers - my Tios - who would sit in lawn chairs in the backyard drinking Coors. I was in catechism at St. Peter Catholic School where I was working on my First Holy Communion. I wasn't fully sold on the concept, but I was looking forward to drinking the wine, and I was dying to know what the flesh of Christ would taste like. I imagined it would be salty like the cookies Mamá made that time she mistook the salt for sugar.

After class I would come home, kick off my uniform and head straight to the kitchen. Mamá, as usual, would be positioned before the stove, cooking something for the men outside. I'd run up from behind and throw my arms around her waist for a quick hug, open the fridge door - BZZZZZT! - grab a few cans of Coors, then run to the backyard to deliver the cold beverages to Papá with his brothers Juan, Jose, and Alberto.

The men often took cover under the shade of the lemon tree. Other times they'd be sitting around the brick stove they built for frying pork skins or cooking up a cow's worth of carne asada. I would hand them their beers and smile when they told me what a good girl I was. I'd linger under the peach trees, pretending to be playing in the dirt but listening to their conversation about so-and-so's cousin's wife running away with the pastor back on the rancho, or telling dirty jokes about a cowboy with a wooden leg. Hearing the clang of empty beer cans being tossed into the pile, I would run back inside and repeat the routine, bringing the next round. This would play out for several hours as the day wore on. With every beer, my Tios became more loopy, the jokes became raunchier and the gossip was so good I would trade it later with my siblings for Bazooka bubble gum or some watermelon Now and Laters.

Next to the refrigerator was a small gas stove suffering from years of overuse. It had four burners, three of which were occupied by our family's staples. For starters, there was the perpetual pot of beans which took up the prime front left burner. If Jesus made the history books by feeding everyone with a few fishes and loaves, Mamá surely outdid him with a handful of beans.

On the front right burner sat the aluminum coffee percolator. I loved to watch as the coffee came to a boil, the dark liquid tossing about in the see-through lid like waves in a tiny brown ocean.

Everyone in the house drank coffee. I enjoyed mine with Carnation®
evaporated milk and heavy doses of sugar - more leche con café than
café con leche.

The third burner at the back left corner housed the comal we
used for cooking the tortillas. This comal had traveled thousands of
miles with Mamá when she married Papá and left her small town in
Mexico. She made the comal out of the trumpet horn from an old
Victrola, smashing it with a hammer to form a round, if not a little
warped, metal plate. The tortillas would always burn in the same
places because of the distinct series of bumps on the surface, leaving
a charred pattern much like a crunchy, delicious fingerprint.

The last of the four burners was the back, right-hand corner
spot. This was the wildcard that featured whatever the meal might
be that day. Sometimes we'd have fideo, or turkey with molé (a
neighborhood favorite), or pork carnitas, and if Papá and the boys
had gone fishing, there'd be sizzling mackerel or catfish stew to go
along with the cold beers. On the dreaded days when Mamá took it
upon herself to make liver and onions, the house would fill with a
stench so bad my siblings and I would flee in all directions as far as
possible, slamming the screen door in disapproval as we dispersed
throughout the street to seek dinner elsewhere.

One weekend out of nowhere, Papá brought home a rabbit.

"For me, Papa?" I asked.

"Yes, mija, please make him as fat as you possibly can," he said with a smile as he took another swig of Coors and looked at my Tios who responded with roars of laughter. As the youngest of the siblings, I had always wanted a younger brother to play with and I figured this was as close as I would get. Elated, I ran inside to grab them another round of Coors.

I could not believe this turn of events and concluded that my years of bringing home gold stars on my quizzes were paying off. I named my new best friend el Tigre del Norte, or Tigger for short, because he was long with orange fur that had a white and brown pattern that looked like stripes. His two front teeth were uneven with one turned slightly inward. I didn't care, I loved his face and his crooked teeth. Tigger and I would run around the backyard, and he would sit next to me on the grass as we watched the clouds go by, picking out those that looked like familiar shapes. Sometimes I sang Tigger songs about Puff the Magic Dragon or read him books like *Charlotte's Web* and *Ramona Quimby*. I even stole my sister's favorite purple hair pick to comb his fur and had to dodge a tennis ball she threw at my head when she found out.

A month went by and I sat in my Saturday catechism class, learning about the different categories of sins. I discovered that no matter what we did, our slate would always be wiped clean by the Lord if we asked him to forgive us. I considered the game-changing implications of this. It seemed like an important sinner's loophole, and I made sure to write this information down, confident that it would come in handy more than once. We wrapped up class with the usual punch and cookies, and I ran home. As I arrived, I could hear the familiar backyard sounds: my Tios tossing their empty beer cans in a pile, and waves of laughter. I ran to my room, shed my uniform, and skipped outside to look for Tigger.

I first gave my saludos, hugging my Tios who were likely on their third round of Coors judging by the pile of empties. I searched for Tigger but he wasn't near the nopal patch, nor was he under the peach trees. He wasn't hiding behind Papá's wooden shed either. I was becoming concerned because these were all his favorite spots. As I walked toward the lemon tree, I noticed there were ropes hanging off the branches, with a puddle of blood in the dirt below. I looked from the ropes to my Tios sitting in their lawn chairs as Papá stood across from them smoking a cigarette. There was blood on his pant legs.

My legs went wobbly at the sight of so much blood. I darted back through the garage and into the house to see if Mamá might know where Tigger was.

She wasn't in her usual spot in the kitchen.

"Mamá! Mamá!" I called out.

Not hearing a response, I stopped in front of the stove.

On the fourth burner sat mamá's large caldo pot. I could hear the liquid inside boiling and observed white wavy curls of steam making their way towards the ceiling. I pulled the chair from the sink over to the edge of the stove. Grabbing the back of the chair as I had done so many times before to lift myself into a standing position,

I leaned my face toward the pot. My nostrils were assaulted with the smell of something like boiling liver. I waved away the steam from my face, pulled my hair back and leaned in further to see what was bobbing around in the water.

I could make out a small but meaty torso, and smallish thighs floating up and down, propelled by big, boiling bubbles. A chicken, maybe? Diced carrots and celery floated past, along with a large onion. Suddenly a small skull bobbed up to the surface and rolled over in the water. I could see two long teeth. Crooked. One shorter than the other.

TIGGER!

I pulled away, my hand gripping the chair so tight I thought my fingers would rip through the vinyl. My brain screamed first before my body kicked in.

I don't know how long I stood screaming with my lungs on full blast.

Then, my Tio walked in laughing to himself and holding something. I turned to him as he approached in slow motion, reaching out to me.

"Mija, this is for you," he said.

My eyes traveled from his weathered face, down his plaid shirt to his outstretched hand. I felt the heat of all the garbage fires of Tijuana burning in my belly.

My Tio was handing me a rabbit's foot.

The fires burning in my pansa went cold, and I felt an ice cube travel up my spine. Everything came into hyperfocus, like the time I watched *The Blob* at the Alondra Six Theatre through a pair of 3D glasses.

I could smell the beer seeping out of my Tio's pores. I could see splatters of blood on his shoes. His smile made my face harden as I clenched my jaw shut.

I jumped off the chair as far away from him as possible, landing hard on my hands and knees. My Tio stepped towards me, attempting to help me up as I crawled backwards away from him, not wanting him to touch me. I stood up and slapped my Tio's hand so hard that the rabbit's foot flew across the kitchen. I began kicking him in the shins as hard as I could with my scuffed but sturdy Buster Browns, as my years of kickball training took over.

A swift kick to the left shin!

Another kick to the right!

My Tio howled in pain which nourished my soul more than any of my catechism prayers ever did. I knew it was a sin to kick my Tio and enjoy it, but I also knew about the Lord's forgiveness loophole which I planned to use later. I kicked him even harder as Papá walked in.

"Que pasa?! Stop it!" he shouted at me.

"Borrachos, you're just a bunch of drunks!" I screamed before turning to run out the front door. In the corner of my eye, I caught Mama standing in her bedroom doorway. I stopped and turned to her. Her eyes were red and puffy, and she was clutching her hands together. I looked at her for a long moment. I thought about Mamá taking care of everyone else, and how taking care of everyone else doesn't mean they will take care of you. I made up my mind that I would never, ever fetch my Tios or anyone else another beer. I turned and ran out of the house, slamming the screen door as I left. I darted past the ficus tree and onto the street, heading north to Courtney's house where I would spend the night, crying to her mom as they consoled me with Hungry-Mans and cherry Kool-Aid. We had fruit salad mixed with whipped cream, coconut, and mini-marshmallows for dessert.

That night as I tried to sleep, I pictured my Tios and Papá fetching their own beers. They would have to make the long walk for themselves. One-by-one, I imagined them walking to the refrigerator.

BZZZZZT! went Tio Juan.

BZZZZZT! went Tio Jose.

BZZZZT! went Tio Alberto.

BZZZZT! went Papá.

Each of the men's shoulders would twitch as they opened the fridge to reach for another round, a current of electricity jolting through their body.

———

THE AFTER-BROTHER, THE BEFORE-BROTHER, AND THE NOW-BROTHER: THE VERY SMALL TELLING OF THE TIME-TRIPLETS OF HONEY, MS

———

by
EXODUS OKTAVIA BROWNLOW
Published in *Wigleaf*

Honey, MS 1938

I . THE AFTER-BROTHER

Mama would not love me.

I reach back to the behind days, to the Before-Brother, who became outside of her body too still. That spanked bottom, way back in that before, the strikes made against skin unsparked, and screams from the Before-Brother funneled into the would-be Mama's mouth—the only after to come from his birth.

The Before-Brother. Oh, she say he was so beautiful, so perfect in his whisper-thin wails, and nowadays Mama can't stand to even hear my smallest whimpers.

She shouts, "Lord, your brother never asked for nothin! Never needed a thing!"

II. THE BEFORE-BROTHER

Mama would not have loved me.

I stretch out to the forward days, to the After-Brother, who bloomed outside of her body squirming.

Those torn scream tones, I touch them, their tastes just the same as my own, had I let them out. No, I held mine on in, fed them to Mama same as she had fed to me, cord to cord, and they just sort of spewed on out from her mouth.

She shouts, shouts at the After-Brother instead of at me, "Lord, take me back! Up out of this after! Take me back! Take me forward! Take me, now!"

III. THE NOW-BROTHER

Mama would have loved you.

I stand still in the ahead days, where Mama is better at mama'ing, to inherit the finest of her affections.

In the ahead days, where time ain't give her no choice but to wring out all of her wrongs. When the body is less *become* and more *abide*, and gets to be quiet, to sit still with all of its done-dids.

Mama reaches back to the After-Brother, stretches out to the Before-Brother, pulls in the Now-Brother, swaddles us all three. She sings— "Lord, look at my mighty-fine children. Mighty-fine! Yesuh, yesuh, all three mighty-fine! I thank Him, I thank ya, I thank Him!"

WILD HOGS
ON THE BACKSIDE
OF YONDER

by
CG CRAWFORD

1997

On that Friday morning, amid the thick, Sweet Lough, Alabama fog, ole man River walked out of the creaking backdoor of his shotgun style home with his mind set on fixing the engine in his 1957 sandstone Cutlass with the help of his best friend Skeeter. But when Lucky and Charm, his two black labs, didn't run up to him upon exiting his house like usual, River knew something was wrong.

He stopped at the edge of his concrete porch steps, looked out into his fourteen acres of land, and whistled for them just as an old blue, rustic Ford pickup truck pulled up to the right side of his property, near the driveway, and honked. Knowing it was Skeeter, River waved at him before turning his attention back to his land in search of his dogs.

Skeeter rolled down a small hill that led to River's car shed. The car shed was to the left of a barn full of equipment and a square-shaped doghouse, both of which River had built by hand some decades ago.

"Lucky . . . Charm!" River called and waited.

Soon, he hoped to see his dogs' legs and paws cut through the weather's bedsheet and greet him with their wagging tails, hanging tongues, and eager bodies. Lucky always said good morning to River by jumping up into his chest, and Charm always greeted him by running around his feet, yearning for a morning treat.

"Lucky . . . Charm?"

River looked toward his field of greens and black-eyed peas on his left. His collards, turnips, and mustards were blooming in the summer air while his black eyes were coming along all thanks to a good rain and special fertilizer he'd bought from the Feed and Seed, one of the few stores still open in the town of three hundred people.

He thought about heading up to the front of his house where two fields of corn sat across from each other, separated by two black-stained fences and an uneven dirt road that Lucky and Charm liked to chase after birds and squirrels. But when River heard Skeeter's Ford engine turn off, and the driver's door open, he decided to head down yonder, towards the doghouse.

"Hey there, now," Skeeter shouted and waved. "Ready to turn this Cutlass out?"

River could barely see Skeeter as he staggered through the fog.

"Say, Skeet! See if ole Lucky and Charm down yonder."

"Alright now," Skeeter said.

River was about to tell of the reason behind his request, but then, somewhere near his field of greens, east of him, he heard a plucking, picking, and chewing sound. The sound stopped River in his tracks. He knew it could only mean one thing: something had died, and another something was eating away at the dead. River walked towards the gnawing with a slight limp and a sharp pain – the kind of pain he charged to arthritis, old age, and six decades worth of labor at the paper mill in Pennington, Alabama, where he had worked until he was seventy-two.

The fog unfolded before him with each step. The reveal of its breaking veil was worse than what River had expected. He expected to see Lucky and Charm, out in the field, dead. Perhaps by way of a mountain lion or a wolf. But what he saw, stretched out across his now desecrated field of greens and black-eyed peas, were the remnants of wild hogs serving as breakfast to a wake of buzzards. "Lord have mercy!" River said.

He swayed his arms across his body as he stepped into the

bloody field. "Go on, get out of here!" he shouted at the eaters of death. Reluctantly, the buzzards dispersed. He wanted to see if Lucky and Charm were among the scattered boar skin. But all he saw, with the buzzards gone, was the tethered state of wild hog heads, guts, and blood webbed in the field of green.

River stood in the center of the slain with his hands on his hips. He wondered what had happened the night before and how he had slept through it. It had to have been the sleeping pill he took. That was the only way he could have slept through such a terror without a flinch or stutter. Lucky and Charm barked in the night. River was sure of it. Intruders on the land, even if it was just a leaf blowing in the wind, always gave sound to their alarm.

Why didn't I hear them? River wondered.

River reached down and picked up one of the half-eaten hog heads by its chipped ear and held it at eye level. He searched for his dogs' teeth marks in its battered skin, even though he knew that the work before him couldn't have been done by his Lucky and Charm. Outside of chasing squirrels, catching rabbits, locating runaway, wounded deer after a morning or evening hunt, and picking up shot-down duck out of the Lilly Grove Lake not too far from the house, Lucky and Charm were more bark than bite. And besides, from what River could tell, the cut around the hog's neck seemed too clean to be the work of canines. No, this was the work of man.

River dropped the hog head to the ground, and then he examined the other bludgeoned hog bodies around him. He looked out at the southernmost part of his property where wild hogs, along with other wild game, were accustomed to coming, going, and eating the corn River often placed out in the acre-long pasture he kept strictly for hunting season.

Deer season was only a few months away.

"Lucky? Charm?" River shouted towards the pasture.

"Over here," Skeeter called from somewhere over yonder.

River hobbled over to the sound of Skeeter's voice, where, just outside the doghouse, Lucky and Charm were on their sides, their front two paws touching. *Dead!*

"Oh no!" River fell to his knees in disbelief. He touched the stiff coat of their skin as tears formed in his eyes. "They ain't gon' is they, Skeet? Tell me they ain't gone."

"Sorry, boss," Skeeter said. "They gone. Can't tell you how long, but they gone."

River shook his head and searched for answers as to how they might've died.

"I don't see no blood," River said, thinking about the wild hogs over in his field of greens and black-eyed peas. "I don't see no blood."

"I noticed that too," Skeeter said. "Maybe they was poisoned."

River ran through the possibilities of fate in his head. "It's a bunch of blood over yonder." River pointed. "All over my black eyes and greens. Wild hogs. Dead. Seem like somebody put them there on purpose."

"You say what now?" Skeeter asked. "Now who would want to do that?"

"A friend of the devil, Skeet. They got to be a friend of the devil."

"Mercy, Lord," Skeeter said. "Mercy."

River tried to pull his dogs closer to him, but his spirit was too weak.

"Ten years, Skeet," River sobbed. "I had ole Lucky and Charm for ten good years."

Skeeter removed the hat on his head and placed it over his heart. "Lucky and Charm been with you ever since you got rid of your horses and cows. Needed someone to keep you and Emma company." Skeeter shook his head. "Who would do such a thing? And to you? That don't make no sense. You don't bother nobody. Hell, ever since Emma died you don't even leave the house but for church. And you barely go there." Skeeter chuckled as if to bring forth an ounce of joy in a time of sorrow.

"I don't know, Skeet. Maybe somebody trying to send a message," River stepped away from Lucky and Charm and looked towards the house with his right hand on his chin.

"There's only one somebody that likes to send a message like this," Skeeter said.

"The McGrangers," River said.

The McGrangers were infamously known all around West Alabama for pushing people off their land for one reason or the other. "What the richest, wealthiest family in all of Sweet Lough want with your land?"

"Ain't no telling," River said. "Ain't no telling."

When River bought the land from Mr. Wilkins in 1963 for one hundred dollars an acre, he just knew that it would be the place to live forever, even in death, where, just outside of the hunting pasture, a plot awaited him next to his wife and his oldest daughter. His land was tucked in the woods of Sweet Lough. The heart of town was seven miles away. The only neighbors he had were birds, trees, and whatever wildlife that loved to nib on his corn and greens. Not even the McGrangers had ever bothered him as they had done to people he knew in, around, and beyond town. Not until now.

"They want your land," Skeeter said. "They put a golf course on Peter James's forty-two acres in Butler, an event center on Thomas Atkins's thirty-seven acres in Sweet Water, and they don' turned Edna Miller's sixty acres in Gilbertown into a hunting club. And that don't even cover half of what they don' done to folks who look like us."

"Mercy, Lord," River said. "Almost thirty-five years on this land with no trouble, and now my name don' reached the top of they list."

"Say, didn't you just come from that Doctor Flucker over in Butler?"

"Yea," River said. "What about him?"

"Well, I just thought about something." Skeeter scratched his chin. 'Peter, Thomas, and Edna? All them was old and sick when they land was so-called sold too. And I think Flucker was they doctor . . . So maybe that's what they doing."

"Doing what?" River asked.

"Ain't Doctor Flucker a distant cousin to the McGrangers?"

"Seem like everybody a distant something to those jokers," River said.

"Well, all I'm saying is it's mighty funny how you was just at the doctor the other day and then a couple days later, your dogs are dead and your field of greens is full of wild hogs. Now, I know we got a wild hog infestation going on 'round here but something in the buttermilk ain't clean about this. It ain't clean one bit."

"Well, I don't understand what you saying," River said. "Now, I might be old, but I ain't sick. Hell, Doctor Flucker said that I was in perfect health. Might even make it to a hundred."

"Think you outta get a second opinion. Can't trust that Dr. Flucker," Skeeter said. "Can't trust nobody with McGranger blood."

River looked over at his dogs and thought about how, just yesterday, Lucky was chasing Charm around the cornfields while he sat on the porch and watched them. And now they were gone. River wasn't much of a crier. The last time he cried was at his wife's funeral. And the time before that was at his daughter's viewing. But here he was now on the verge of a third cry in twenty years. River raised his right index finger up to his left eye and tried to keep the water from going beyond its holding place.

"I want to call the Sheriff, but I know that joker ain't gon' do nothing."

"Nall," Skeeter said. "Sheriff Cunningham got McGranger blood too. Hell, that's how he got the job. 'Cause he sholl nuff ain't get in on merit."

"I want you to call ole Rickey Taylor and Bozeman," River said. "Tell them to bring their rifles. We gon' clean up, give Lucky and Charm a nice burial down yonder, and then we gon' see if the McGrangers bold enough to come back 'round here."

"Roger that," Skeeter said. "Let me go get my phone out the truck."

"Alright," River said. "The McGrangers have been getting away with this for long enough. It's about time somebody put their foot down. And that somebody gon' be us."

• • •

Ten minutes later, Bozeman and Rickey Taylor rushed down River's long dirt road in a blue Chevrolet truck. Rickey Taylor jumped out of its passenger side well before the four-wheel drive came to a complete stop down the hill on the backside of River's land. "Where they at?" Rickey Taylor asked as he cocked his rifle. "Where those motherfuckers at?" He walked like a cowboy carrying a gun that was too heavy for him to hold.

"Slow down before you blow a hip out of place," Skeeter said to Rickey Taylor while holding the hearse that River asked him to grab from the barn for Lucky and Charm. The hearse was a wheel barrel. "Them jokers long gone."

"Is it true?" Bozeman asked as he walked over towards the ole men with his .30-30 in hand. "They took my Lucky?" Lucky was his favorite of the two labs. He reminded Bozeman of a lab he used to have before a venomous snake bite called him home. His name was Charlie.

"I'm afraid so, Boze," River said while standing next to one of his tractors. "And they left me a little message over yonder. A bunch of hog heads and tethered bodies."

"Didn't know it was that much evil in the world," Rickey Taylor said and shook his head.

"If them dogs barked one time. I mean just one time at any point of the night, I'd usually wake up, you know? But I reckon last night was different. 'Cause last night? I ain't hear no Lucky. And I ain't hear no Charm."

"You the third person this month," Rickey Taylor said, leaning the rifle on his side to grab a cigarette out of his plaid shirt pocket. "I talked to Ole Boon the other day over there in Sumter County. He said them McGrangers did something similar to his cornfield. But instead of cutting up hogs and killing dogs, they used horse shit to send their message. Spread it all on his corn. And I ain't talkin' about the ground. I ain't talkin' fertilizer. I'm talkin' shuffled corn with horse shit on it like it's some kind of cream. And yall know how shit get when the sun hit. All stiff and thangs? They did it in the night . . . when nobody was watching."

River and the men shook their heads.

"I wonder who his doctor is," Skeeter said, more to himself than anyone else.

"A couple days later," Rickey Taylor continued. "They came back 'round Ole Boon talkin' about how their horses on Cousin So and So land had got out and ran wild. Said that they might keep coming back unless he sold his land for a dollar an acre. Can you believe that? A dollar an acre?"

"What did Ole Boone say?" River asked.

"He told the McGrangers that they could kiss his ass."

The men let out a sober chuckle. River included.

"Where he at now?" Bozeman asked, curious and smiling.

"The Traveling Shoes Funeral Home." Rickey Taylor said. There was a crack in his voice. "His funeral next Saturday at Morning Star Baptist Church in Little, Walker."

"Lord have mercy." Skeeter said. "Say it ain't so."

River looked at Skeeter with a wonder in his soul.

"Bless his name," Bozeman said.

"His son found him dead just the other day," Rickey Taylor said. "Apparently, he died in his sleep."

"Lord have mercy," Skeeter said before the men stood in silence for a few seconds.

"What do you want to do?" Rickey Taylor looked to River. River let out a breath of uncertainty. Then he told Bozeman to follow him down the hill to bury Lucky and Charm while Skeeter and Rickey Taylor tended to the mess of wild hogs in the field of black-eyed peas and greens. "I was gon' burn them hogs, but I don' changed my mind." River turned to look at his house. "I want yall to preserve what's left of the buzzards' feast and bring them to the barn. We gon' wash the blood off them and keep what we can."

"What you want to do that for?" Skeeter asked.

"'Cause," River smiled. "The McGrangers sent a message, and I'm gon' send one right back."

• • •

The men did everything that ole man River asked them to do. And after burying the dogs, and scooping up pieces of the wild hogs, River brought out a green sowing kit that belonged to his wife and placed it on a table in the barn. There, River took the flesh remnants of the wild hogs and used black and red thread to create three hog head masks that looked like the work of an untrained slasher artist. "Abracadabra! Wallakazam!" River shouted as he lifted the heads up and showed them to the men. "What do you think?"

"Huh . . . that's some fine taxidermy you got there, River," Skeeter said. The tone in his voice lacked the authority that sometimes came with telling the truth.

"Huh . . . River, don't take this the wrong way, but . . . huh . . . if you had a day job, I'd tell you to keep it," Rickey Taylor said while trying to hold his laughter.

"What you gon' do with that?" Bozeman asked.

River rose from the table where he'd just conducted taxidermy surgery, and then he asked Skeeter, Rickey Taylor, and Bozeman to grab three long metal stakes that were sitting against the barn wall, and a shovel. "Might need the tractor to get them, but when you do, I want you to bring them up to the cornfields. That's where I'm gon' put them."

"Oh, I see where you going with this," Skeeter said with a smile.

"Careful with them stakes now. They be kind of heavy."

"We got it, old man," Rickey Taylor said. "You just head on up.

River chuckled on his way out of the barn with the masks in his hands. Soon, the men came around the bend of River's house with the metal bars on his tractor. The stakes were about twenty feet long. All the men worked together to remove the stakes one by one from the tractor, and then they placed them in the cornfield to the right of the house but facing the dirt road. River dug holes three feet apart from each other with enough depth to help the stakes withstand strange weather and strong winds. Then he placed the distorted hog heads on the stakes before the men helped raise them up, put them in the ground, covered the hole up, and patted it down.

Above their heads and the corn itself, stood three monstrous hog heads that looked like a bunch of scarecrows. "Them sholl nuff is some ugly heads," Skeeter said.

"Sholl nuff is," Rickey Taylor said. "Sholl nuff is."

"It's gon' be the first thing anybody see when they pull on your property." Bozeman said.

"This will be their warning," River said. "Next time them jokers want to come around here acting like animals, I'm gon' treat them like one. I'm gon' beat 'em like they stole something, and then I'm gon'e place these masks over their heads."

"Right on," Skeeter said. "Right on."

• • •

For the next few days, Skeeter, Rickey Taylor, and Bozeman hung out around River's house, canvassing, listening, and monitoring the land with their rifles in hand, waiting for the McGrangers to reappear. Word had spread around town about what the McGrangers had done on River's property, especially on that following Sunday when Bozeman and Taylor, deacons at Greater Word Missionary Baptist Church, hadn't showed up for service, and at the bingo hall on Highway Ten, where Skeeter was a regular. When Mrs. Taylor came around the bend, to the back porch, where the men were sitting, with Sunday dinner – hammocks, collard greens, baked macaroni and cheese, potato salad, and sweet potato pie – she told River that folks had come by to see him, but those hog heads in the front forced them to turn around for fear of what would happen to them if they entered his property. "Yea, we been seeing folks pull up and turn around," Skeeter said and laughed. "Thought I saw Mr. Jankin's car earlier this morning out there."

"Yea, that was him," Mrs. Taylor said and laughed. "He said he had come by here. But when he saw them heads, he came right on to church and went straight to the altar for prayer. And I can't tell you when the last time Jankin's came to church. But when I saw them hog heads for myself? I understood. Them heads would make anybody want to give their life back to Christ. Don't matter if they already gave it to him once. Them heads will make you want to do it again."

"As long as it keep them McGrangers away from River's property, then all is well," Bozeman said. "But, River, if it's helping folks like Jankin give his life over to God, then Pastor Tolbert outta give you a piece of that offering he gets every other Sunday. Everybody knows Jankin is a heathen."

The men laughed, and Mrs. Taylor did too.

"Thank you for this food, Sister Taylor," River said. "Remind me of my Emma."

"Yes, Lord," Mrs. Taylor said. "We all miss her. Her and your oldest daughter."

"Lord knows I miss them," River said. "Bethany and Benjamin miss them too. They don't come down here no more, or call me like they used to, but I know they miss their mother and sister like I do."

"How long has it been since you seen them?"

"Sister, I couldn't call it if I tried. My memory gets all fuzzy these days. But I know it's been a while." River said. "I reckon I'll be joining my Emma pretty soon, especially if these McGranger jokers get their way. I'd rather die than let these jokers run me off my own property." River took a sip of the sweet tea that Mrs. Taylor had brought with the meal.

"Oh, don't speak that way," Mrs. Taylor said. "God's gon' get the final say. Yes, sir, indeed. The Lord is gon' work this thing out."

"Yea," Skeeter said. "We ain't gon' let nothin' happen to you, River. We got your back."

"Yea, River, you gon' make it to a hundred years old," Bozeman said and laughed. River smirked at the thought. He touched the center of his chest and massaged the bump that sat just over his heart. "Maybe so," River said. "Maybe so."

"Make it so, Lord! Make it so!" Mrs. Taylor said in an elevated voice. She lifted her hands and tilted her head towards the sky as if she was still in church.

"Speaking of the McGrangers," Rickey Taylor rose from the chair he was sitting in on the back porch. "Let me take you home 'case these fools try to pop out on you on the way back."

"I would like that," Mrs. Taylor said. Then, before heading back to the car, she told River that the whole church was praying for him. River expressed his everlasting gratitude – once more for the food, and then for the prayers too.

"I'll be back 'round here, River," Rickey Taylor said.

"Nall, you've done more than enough. Matter of fact, all of you have." River dusted his hands and stood up. "It's Sunday. Yall should go home." Skeeter and Bozeman tried to object but River wouldn't hear of it. "This the Lord's day. Not my day," River said. "Bozeman, your daughter is probably worried sick about you now that the word is out. And Skeeter – don't you got some women to tend to down there at the bingo hall?" The men laughed before caving into River's demands, shaking hands, and leaving the back porch. "First sign of trouble? Call. You hear?" Skeeter said before heading to his truck.

"You have my word," River said. Then he watched as the men and Mrs. Taylor drove off in their cars and trucks in a single line down the dirt road. Their cars faded as their tires picked up dirt and left a cloud of dust on their trail. River looked on until the vehicles were out of sight and out of reach of him and the hogs' empty eyes.

• • •

On the next day, River woke up with the goal of working on that Cutlass engine. He and Skeeter hadn't had time to tend to it after the McGrangers's hog-like tactics, but River was ready to reclaim the narrative over his own time and space. Before heading down to the car shed, he had planned to sit out on the front porch with a cup of black coffee in hand, but when he opened the front door and saw a tan GMC trailblazer, where two men sat in the front seat, parked just beyond the hog heads, his plans changed. River always kept a rifle by the front door, so he dropped his morning coffee, grabbed the rifle, angled it towards the truck, and started firing without thought or question. First it was his coffee mug shattering on the concrete ground of his porch, and then it was the sound of bullets jumping out from his rifle as he stepped down from the porch and towards the truck with each shot. The man in the driver's seat placed the truck in reverse and hightailed it out of River's range. River didn't stop shooting, even after they were gone. He had been shooting over the truck the whole time, but he wanted his lingering shots to register like fire in the bones.

After standing and watching the road for a while, River closed his eyes and took a deep breath. "I'm tired, Lord," he said. "I'm so tired."

River looked up at the hog-head stakes. They were still intact, looking on, eyeless. Bugs had begun to swarm around the masks as if to eat of its remaining flesh. River decided not to call Skeeter, Bozeman, and Rickey Taylor on his way back inside the house. He wanted to focus on getting the Cutlass up and running. And so he did. "I'm not going to let these jokers stop me from living on my land," River said as he prepared to head down yonder to his car shed. "No sir, I am not."

• • •

That same evening, River was working under the carriage of his Cutlass with the help of his blue creeper and a wrench when two men snuck up on him with hunting rifles in their hands.

"You got a nice car there," a voice said in the space between the inclined cement that separated the grass from the shed's floor. River bumped his head on an organ of the car once he heard the voice.

"Awh!" River said as he slid from under the car's belly while a small, hard knot, the size of a pecan, formed on the top right side of his forehead.

"Careful there," a man with red hair and brown freckles said. "That might hurt in the morning." The man with red hair smiled as he stood next to a heavyset man wearing a plaid blue and white shirt with dip in his mouth.

River stared at the men for more than a second. There was something about them that seemed familiar. And then River remembered: These were the men who had been watching him from the road in that GMC trailblazer. River shook his head and laughed. More at himself than the men in front of him. "You gentlemen lost?" River asked.

He reached down to his right and grabbed the greasy red rag sitting on top of his CRAFTSMAN toolbox. First, he dabbed his forehead with it, and then he brought the rag down to his eyes to check for blood within the black smut, but there was none.

"I don't think so," the man with red hair said. "I think we right where we need to be, especially seeing how your goons aren't here to protect you."

"Goons? You talkin' 'bout my dogs? Or are you talkin' 'bout the men you been waiting to leave just to come see about ole River?" River hoped to get a confession from the men about them killing Lucky and Charm, even if it was the last thing he'd ever do.

"Is there a difference between the two?" the man with the red hair asked. "Dogs? Men? When it comes to folks like you, aren't yall all the same?"

River looked over at the rifle leaning against the table across from him. The rifle was sitting next to the small vintage television that hadn't been plugged up in almost thirty years. And even though he wouldn't be able to reach it before the man with red hair, or the man with the thick stomach, shot him, he thought to go for it anyway.

"Take it easy, now," the man with red hair said. "Listen, I am Red. This here is Big Jim. And we come in peace."

River tightened the grip on the wrench in his left hand and stepped towards the men as if he was the one holding a deadly weapon.

"You call killing my dogs and destroying my field of greens and black-eyes coming in peace?" River gritted his teeth.

"Look to me like a bunch of wild hogs did that," Red said, and Big Jim laughed.

"Yea," River said. "I'm looking right at them hogs you speak of."

An uncomfortable silence stood between River and the men

as they continued to measure each other up. Then Big Jim spat onto the concrete of the car shed.

Red turned to look out at the land while Big Jim kept his eyes on River. "Ever thought about selling?"

"Selling? Oh no! I can't do that," River scoffed. "This here land ain't for sell."

"Oh, come on. Name your price. Everybody's got a price."

River chuckled and shook his head. "See there? You not understanding me." River took another step towards the men. "This here is family land. I'm leavin' this land to my children, and their children, and their children's children." River smiled. "This here land ain't for sale."

"You sure about that?" Red asked and tilted his head.

"Boy, what part of 'No!' don't you understand?" River raised up the wrench in his hand.

Big Jim tightened his grip on his rifle. Then he licked his lips as if he was hungry for blood.

"Now I don' told you: this land ain't for sale. So, I reckon you two best be on your way and have a good day."

"Listen, ole man," Red said, leaning forward. "You got some interests of ours, and we want to make you a deal."

"Interests? What interests of mine you got?"

"We want that pasture you got back yonder," Big Jim said before Red could speak. "You know . . . where you do your killing."

"My pasture?'

"Yea," Red said. "Seem like our hogs been drifting over onto this side of town more and more each year, and we figured we'd offer you something for that pasture back there. But then we saw the land and said why not just offer you a deal for all the land. After all, word is that bump you got in the center of your chest is more than a bump. And you ain't too kind to medicine. And your family ain't been back here in quite some time. So you might as well sell."

"Now wait just a damn minute," River said in disbelief. "Where you get all that mess you talking about? Flucker say something to you about me and mine? What the hell Flucker doing telling my business? Thought that was private information?"

"What about the pasture?" Red asked, ignoring River's questions. "Won't you just sell us that part of the land? It's not like you hunt as much as you used to anyway."

"You been watching me?" River asked. "How long yall been watching me?"

River took a step back as if he was thinking about their proposal. But he was actually trying to figure out how long they had had their eyes on him. River touched his chest as if to think of what Skeeter had said about his doctor and the McGrangers. "You know," he said and pointed towards the pasture. "If yall were to buy that part of the land, then yall would have to come 'cross this land—back and forth, back and forth." River made big circles with the wrench in his hand. "Now, given that the Jemisons own the land between me and the land where yall trying to hunt them hogs . . . and given how I know yall ain't gon' be able to persuade the Jemisons to cut a trail from that backside of the woods to the main road, you'd have to come through this way –" River pointed to the front entrance of his property. "And I can't have that." River shook his head. "Nall, yall gon' be riding them John Brown four wheelers, tearing up my grass and running through my fields like yall ain't got good sense. And I can't have that."

Red and Big Jim looked at each other with a smirk as if their proposals weren't proposals at all. "You know we can take your land off your hands by force if we wanted to, don't you?"

Red and Big Jim raised their rifles up to River's chest and held it there.

River laughed before lining up to the men as if he had a gun on his hip. River couldn't help but to think about his family as he tried to stand firm. His back was drenched in sweat. "I used to be afraid to die. Didn't want to leave the world too early for fear of what I could miss. Then I lost my wife, and then my oldest daughter. And after you lose two of the biggest loves of your life, you soon learn that death ain't nothing to fear." River shook his head. "No, death becomes a kind of desire, a yearning if you will."

River stepped into the barrel of Big Jim's rifle as if to dare him to shoot.

Red nudged Big Jim and told him it was time to go. Big Jim held the rifle to River's chest for a second longer. River could feel the barrel on the lump just over his heart. When Big Jim lowered his gun, he spat a brown loogie at River's feet.

"We'll be back, Ole Man." Red laughed.

"That's fine! Just be sure to call first," River said. "Maybe then I'll have some tea cakes waiting on you when you come back." River watched the two men walk into the woods. "Hey," River shouted while pointing the wrench at the men. Red and Jim looked back. "You see them hog heads out front?" River asked. "Next time you jokers come onto my property. I'm gon' replace them hog heads with your heads. You hear?"

"Judging by the way you shoot, we ain't got nothing to worry about," Red said, laughing before the two men entered the woods, heading west.

"It's called a warning shot, motherfucker." River shouted as he watched the men fade beyond the leaves and oak trees. "Next time won't be no warning."

• • •

Later in the afternoon, River grabbed his rifle and called Skeeter, Rickey Taylor, and Bozeman. He told the men to come back to his property without delay, where, that night, they'd wait for the McGrangers to return. The men met between the barn and the doghouse.

"Can't believe you ain't call us this morning," Skeeter said before the men dispersed to their designated spots upon their arrival.

"Yea, River," Bozeman said, holding his .270. "You know we would have come 'round here just as soon as you called."

"I know," River said. "I just didn't want to bother you with it. I was hoping these folks would just go away, even though I knew they wouldn't." A sense of sorrow held on to River's voice. "We too old for this. Too old."

The men nodded, even though they felt as if there was nothing else they could do but wait and fight. Bozeman recommended calling more people, but River rejected the request. "It's too dangerous," River said. "Hopefully we will be enough."

The men stood in silence for a moment, looking at each other.

Rickey Taylor had brought a bag with him. The bag had extra ammo in it, but it also had a bunch of cookies in foil wrap. "The wife made them for us to snack on while we watch and wait . . . and pray," Rickey Taylor said. "She praying too. Lord knows she is."

He handed each man a foil wrap with three cookies inside it.

The men nodded at each other before heading to their spots. Rickey Taylor went south, down by the hunter's house, where the wild hogs often appeared. Bozeman went west, across from the field of greens and black-eyed peas. Skeeter stayed there, east of the property, and pulled out a chair from the car's shed to sit between the barn and the doghouse. And River headed back up to the house to assume his position on the porch to watch the road.

"Hey, River," Skeeter called before sitting down. River turned to look back at him.

"Yea, Skeet?"

"You called your children lately? Told them what's going on?"

River shook his head. "Nall," he said. "I ain't want to burden them with this stuff . . . You know they got busy lives in the cities they living in. Chicago . . . Los Angeles . . ."

"Yea," Skeeter said. "Maybe so . . . but then again, maybe you outta give 'em a call." River let Skeeter's words digest as they looked at each other with a knowing sense.

"Huh . . . yea, Skeet. Maybe you right."

"Alright, now," Skeeter said. "Just call."

River nodded. "I will," he said. "I will."

• • •

Once River made it to the front porch and sat down in his rocking chair with his rifle over his lap, he used his landline to call his daughter first, and then his son. Both calls rang and rang and rang before going to voicemail.

On the second call, the one to his son, a beep signaled for River to speak.

So, he did.

"Huh . . . Hey son," River said. He was still unsure of whether to tell about the McGrangers. "How is it going? Hope my favorite daughter-in-law and grandchildren are doing alright." River coughed. "I huh . . . I just called to give you some bad news . . . Huh . . . Lucky and Charm don' died. Yea . . . huh . . . a bunch of hogs did it. Wild hogs. But don't worry, son. I'm gon' get'em. Yes sir, I'm gon' kill 'em dead."

River went to hang up the phone inside the house, and then he came back, sat down, and readjusted the rifle in his lap. He placed his right hand just above the trigger and leaned back in his chair. He used his free left hand to work a chocolate chip cookie from the foil and ate it slowly, savoring each bite. The sun was on its way down. River kept his eyes on the dirt road, knowing that, if his gut was right, the night would end in one hell of a fight. He was tired, but he had no plans of falling asleep. But as the day faded, and the night came, so, too, did River. He faded into a dream, where, out in the cornfields, he heard the voices of Lucky and Charm, calling out to him. River looked up and saw them running towards the front porch in a veil of white light, and he called back out to them – with tears in his eyes.

DOLLHOUSES

by
MONIC DUCTAN
Published in *Kweli Journal*

It's a Sunday morning, and I'm driving home from brunch. I get stuck behind one of those big, obnoxious trucks with a "wide load" sign on it. The thing about Knoxville is that you have to share the interstate with all kinds of trucks, and as you incline they have trouble shifting gears. The left lane clogs up with cars, so I follow the monstrous truck at a safe distance. It's hauling one half of a double-wide trailer. One of the trailer's windows is positioned in my line of sight, and I can see straight through the house. There's counter space on one side, and on the wall facing me there're holes for a washer and dryer. Trailer designs have come a long way since I was a girl. I grew up in a double-wide with a tin roof, green carpet, and walls paneled in dark, knotty wood.

I grow impatient with the slow crawl along the interstate, so I get off at the next highway to take the back roads home. October is the only right answer when asked which month is best. It's warm enough, and afternoons like this one are breezy and bright. The leaves have turned yellow and red and orange. A row of ducks moves slowly over the water as I cross the bridge leading into my subdivision. Today the water is a swampy brown color, and it has little ripples in it.

I don't see the boy until I come too fast around a curve and nearly sideswipe him. He scurries into a ditch by the side of the road. He's about twelve years old and Black, maybe mixed-race. As I drive by him, I see the scared look on his face. His eyes are widened, and his shoulders are drawn up to his ears.

Slowing down to a crawl, I realize that nearly being taken out by my car is not what has him so scared. He's looking up the hill to where an older Black boy in a black hoodie is standing. The boy in the hoodie yells something to the scared boy, though I can't make out the words. I go down a few yards and pull into my driveway. I hop out of the car and call out to the boy, "Hey! You okay?"

He pants, as if he's just been running. Without a word, he nods.

I approach the scared boy. "You sure?" I ask, following his line of sight to the older kid on the hilltop. The older one looks like he's maybe late teens or early twenties.

"I'm fine," the boy says. He's shaking, and the palm of his hand is up against the side of his face. When he moves his hand away, I see the swelling beneath one of his eyes. His face is streaked with tears. The boy has light brown skin and a long face with heavy eyebrows. As I move to put a hand on his shoulder, he tears his eyes away from the boy on the hill and starts moving away from me.

"Slow *down*," I say, my voice sharp, the way I speak when I'm daring one of my own children to test my patience. My kids have grown up and moved away, but that doesn't mean I can't command a child to do my bidding.

He comes to a complete stop and turns toward me, waiting for me to catch up.

"Is that your brother?" I ask.

"Who?" he asks.

I turn to point behind me to the boy on the hill, but the older boy has suddenly disappeared. There are trees up on the ridge, and houses beyond that.

I turn back to the boy in front of me.

"Do you know that kid on the hill?"

He stares at me a long while, and for a moment I worry that he's slow or has trouble understanding me. He shakes his head. "No, ma'am," he says.

It's been a long while since I've been called ma'am by a child. I've got three grandbabies and their parents don't press those little niceties.

"You look familiar to me," I tell him. He looks a lot like my grandson Bobby—the same big brown eyes, the same way of ducking their heads down when they think they're in trouble.

"What's your name?" I ask.

"They call me 'Son,' but I'm Michael, or Little Michael."

"Which do you prefer?"

His eyebrows shoot up in surprise, as if no one has ever asked him such a thing before. "Son, I guess," he says.

He starts to walk away, and even though I've lived in this neighborhood thirty years and never had any problems, I'm worried about a child wondering around alone, especially one who has just been jumped on.

"Where do you live?" I ask.

He turns to look at me again, and I wonder if he thinks I'm trying to give him a hard time or being too nosy.

"Up at Rosewood," Son says, pointing up the hill near the direction his attacker walked.

Rosewood is a pay-by-the-week motel in a dingy stucco building with a parking lot that needs recementing. If Son goes home, he could be beaten again, which is probably why he's walking toward the church instead of up the hill. My heart speeds up a little.

"If you'll trust me, I'll take you back to my house and get an ice pack for that eye."

He looks me up and down. If I were him, I'm not sure I'd go into a stranger's house.

"I've got lunch meat. I could make you a sandwich and give you some cookies." *God*, I sound like a pedophile luring a child into a van with a fistful of candy.

But Son nods and steps toward me.

As we walk to my house, Son keeps looking up the hill toward Rosewood. The look of timidity in his eyes breaks my heart.

The homes in this neighborhood are all two and three stories tall and made of partial brick. We enter my house and I lead him back to the kitchen.

"I have turkey and ham," I say. "Which do you like? Or, I could do tuna salad."

I'm not sure if Son heard me. Rather than answer, he looks around at the granite countertops and shaker cabinets. He runs his hand slowly over the smooth surface of the kitchen table. He makes his way to the dollhouse on the countertop above the dishwasher.

I collect dollhouses. I have a spare bedroom full of them and not much room for this new one that sits here in the kitchen. This dollhouse is painted white. What I love most about it are the pale blue window shutters and the furniture. A blue settee and a baby blue carpet take up a sizable part of the living room space. The kitchen has a chandelier made of shiny plastic adorned with tiny yellow and white rhinestones.

"Where did you get this?" Son asks, his eyes wide. He looks up at me as if to ask permission before lightly placing a finger on the little chandelier. The chandelier swings back and forth, spilling light on the ceiling and sending shadows down the walls.

"I got it online, but I used to order the wood and build them with my kids when they were little," I tell him. "It's not difficult. You just have to measure the dimensions and sand things down."

I pick up the dollhouse and take it over to the kitchen table so that Son can sit and play with it. He starts moving the furniture around the dollhouse. My grandson won't play with dollhouses or dolls. He calls them "girl toys." But Son is different. He leans forward and touches everything so delicately.

I pull open the freezer and grab an ice pack. I wrap the cold plastic pack in a warm dish towel and hand it to Son. He holds the pack to his eye with one hand and plays with the dollhouse furniture with his other hand.

My dog Buster leaps up the patio steps and comes to the sliding glass door of the kitchen.

He puts a paw on the glass and scratches.

Now I remember where I've seen Son before. Months ago, Buster and I were sitting on the patio in the backyard. I have several apple trees back there, and one day two kids jumped the back fence. One was this boy, Son, and the other was a young girl who looked similar to him—the same light brown skin and long face. They must be brother and sister. The girl held out the front of her dress and dropped several apples into it, a smart way to carry them. Buster, who lay at my feet on the patio, sat up from his nap and started barking at the kids. They looked up and saw us and took off running toward the fence. Buster started to run after them, but I called him back. He continued to yelp. The girl fell, and then Son, stealing a glance over his shoulder at Buster and me, helped her to her feet. They ran off with the apples.

Now Son stares at the dollhouse chandelier, his eyes gleaming. He puts his finger on the chandelier again and makes it teeter back and forth. He adjusts one of the chairs in an upstairs room and then slides it over in front of the window seat.

"Are you hungry?" I ask him.

He looks up at me and nods. "I didn't have any lunch."

Did he not have any lunch because he hasn't gotten around to it yet, or did he not have lunch because there is no food at his place? I think of the apples he once stole from my yard, and I wonder if he was hungry that day, too. The apples back there never amount to much good. They're usually wormy and they taste nothing like a good Red Delicious apple from the market. Still, I suppose if you pick the right ones they will sustain a hungry child for a little while.

"Am I in some trouble or something?" he asks. He looks back and forth between me and the dollhouse.

"No," I say, my voice cracking with emotion. "Would you like a sandwich or would you like something else?"

He stands up and goes to the fridge where he puts his hand on the door handle and looks at me. I nod my consent, and he pulls open the door and starts to go through the fridge. He pulls out sandwich meat, cheese, pickles, mustard, a pack of Oreos, a bottle of Coke, and a flat of strawberries, and lines it all up on the counter. "Can I fix it myself?"

"Of course," I say. "Wash your hands first."

I point toward the bathroom out in the hallway, but he grabs the dish soap on the lip of the sink, squirts it into his palm and washes his hands there at the sink. I pull a dish towel from a kitchen drawer and offer it to him, but he's already drying his hands on the front of his cargo shorts. I stuff the towel back into the drawer and take a seat at the table to watch him build his lunch. Son takes a plate from the drying rack by the sink. "Got some bread?" he asks, and I point to the bread box by the stove. His hands move quickly. "Knife?" he says, pantomiming the motion he will make to smear the mustard over the bread. I point to the drawer by the dishwasher.

When he's done making his lunch, Son doesn't stop to put the food back in the fridge.

Instead, he brings his plate over to the table. It's piled up with two sandwiches, a handful of strawberries, and two stacks of Oreos on the very edge of the plate.

I get up to put the leftover food away. At some point I glance over at him. He's eating with full attention, stuffing one bite into his mouth and hardly chewing before taking another bite. Watching Son eat is reminiscent of watching my brother Alton back when we were kids. Our family would have food at the start of each week, but by the time Wednesday or Thursday rolled around food was scarce. We'd yearn for Friday when Mama and Daddy would get paid again. My brother Alton was a fat kid, not because we were always well-fed, but because he gorged himself on the days when we had plenty of food. Watching Son eat, I see that he probably has some type of food insecurity. He's tall for his age but looks a little thin. Maybe he doesn't get good meals often.

He pauses and holds his hand to his stomach, and I can tell he's trying not to belch loudly. Still, a soft burp escapes from his lips.

"Do you wanna take the rest of that home with you?"

He nods enthusiastically. I give him a paper plate and some plastic wrap and he dumps the second sandwich and some cookies onto the plate.

"You know what?" I say. "Why don't you take that flat of strawberries and those other Oreos with you?" I step over to the fridge and pull the food out. I pile it into a plastic bag and hand it to him.

"Thanks," he says, and then hurriedly he asks, "Do you want me to go home now, or can I play with your dollhouse some more?"

"You can stay," I tell him. "But I also want you to tell me what happened to you."

Son is looking down at the dollhouse. He keeps his head lowered but moves his eyes up to look at me.

"Are you afraid to go home?"

He shakes his head no, but I can see the truth in his sad eyes.

"If you're scared, you can tell me. We can call someone to help you."

He shakes his head. "They don't help."

I don't ask who "they" are, but I can imagine who "they" are. Probably social services. Police. "Look, if you ever need anything, come to this house." My voice cracks on every other word. Tears spill from Son's eyes. He puts his head face down on the table, and I pat his back. There's a knock at the door.

I squeeze Son's shoulder and head to the living room to answer the door. I find Hank

Baker on the front porch in his blue policeman's uniform. Hank is the son of a man I went to school with years ago. The Bakers all go to my church.

"Hey, Miss Christine," he says to me. "I got a call about two boys fighting in the road." He gestures down the street toward the cul-de-sac. "I talked to one of your neighbors who said he saw a boy come home with you. Is he still here?"

My heart sinks a little. If Son were nervous to talk to me, I can only imagine how he'll feel to speak to a cop. Besides, Hank would probably take him home, and I'm not sure if Son will even be safe there. "He's here," I whisper to Hank. "He was jumped on by an older boy, and he's scared."

I hear the sliding glass door open in the kitchen. "Hang on," I tell Hank.

I rush through the living room and back to the kitchen. The sliding door stands wide open, and Son's kitchen chair is empty.

"Miss Christine?" Hank calls out as he follows me to the kitchen. I go over to the sliding door and watch Son disappear through the fence gate.

Hank is talking, but I can't focus on his words. I close the sliding door and sit down in the seat vacated by Son. The dollhouse has been left in disarray with one chair overturned and the TV stand keeling over against the wall on two legs.

Nothing bad ever happens in a dollhouse. The toy people sit in front of TVs and recline on beds. They are, of course, modeled after us humans. Yet there are so many of us who wish we could step into those houses where everything is picturesque, safe.

MIDDLING

by
LATANYA MCQUEEN
Published in *Pleiades*

Martin was the one to bring it up, pointing out the sign as they drove by. The board depicted an outline of their state divided into two parts, the acronym CWRA emboldened across the image. She'd glanced at the billboard and then forgot about it like she had the numerous other signs that perpetuated the town, signs advertising Bible conventions or gun shows.

She should have known then he'd had a reason for bringing it up. He'd been trying to tell her. For the past few months Martin had been taking part in a group called the "Civil War Re-enactors

Association," preparing to perform what the group called living histories or attempts at recreating certain historical events.

"Why?" It was the only question Candace could muster when he finally told her. Martin had never been in the military and to her knowledge never had an interest in history. He preferred watching reruns of comedy sitcoms to documentaries. A quite, mild-mannered man, he worked as a manager of Clark's Grocery, a job come spring he'd have for the past fifteen years. His job held the same expectations and pitfalls. Every day was more or less the same—he worked the day shift, going in to open at five each morning and staying until the late afternoon. He wore the same plaid shirts and creased trousers, shined his brown loafers each night. She couldn't imagine him, with his particular rituals and daily habits, to want to spend his free days or even hours in some grassy field and dressed in an elaborate 19th century costume.

"It's just a hobby," Martin shrugged, "nothing to get bent out of shape about."

"But why not bowling or fly-fishing? A person doesn't wake up one morning and decide this is something they've always wanted to do."

"Maybe I did Candace. You don't know."

When Candace was a teenager, her mother had always advised her to marry a kind, boring man. A man who loves you more than you love him so that he'll spend the years of the marriage making up the difference. While in college she'd taken her mother's advice and found Martin. After graduation they got married and he moved her back to his hometown in Missouri. Candace hadn't minded her boredom at first because she thought soon they'd have kids, but years of trying followed by the blame for why it never happened, had caused them to drift. Without kids, their life became an endless stream of what they'd had before, and somehow, now that she was nearing forty and looking back on the years of her life, she'd expected more.

Listening to Martin, Candace learned a lot about reenactments. The calvary he was affiliated with didn't just reenact battles but created fictional ones that never happened during the war but they felt, could have. They came up with hypothetical scenarios and reenacted the outcomes using the strategies, uniforms, weaponry and military structure from both the Confederate and Union sides. Reenactments were more than just battles—whole weekends were devoted to this, and during that time members spent the days doing what they imagined actual soldiers did. They practiced tactics to use in upcoming battles. They gambled, played games, and wrote letters to family. They sat by fires cooking meals and talking.

"What about food?" Candace asked, trying to be involved.

"Sure," Martin nodded. "Hardtack mostly, salted pork and dried peas."

Martin took his confession to Candace and her half-hearted interest as liberty to not just purchase what he wanted but parade it around. It appeared as if he'd bought the entire catalogue from whatever store sold such merchandise. Gone were the magazines and photography books that'd normally sat on their coffee table. Books like *Artillery Tactics for the Confederate Man* and *Rules for the Care and Cleaning of the Rifle Musket* took their place. To get used to his costume, Martin wore it when he wasn't at work—cotton trousers and his issued shirt made from unbleached muslin. He had two uniform fatigue jackets that he alternated wearing, each lined with interior pockets.

Martin didn't shower on the days he wore his re-enactor clothes despite his internal desire to keep them new. His plastic-framed reading glasses he kept hidden inside their beside drawer, preferring blurry vision to being what he called, a Farby, a type of imposter, someone with historically inaccurate items or clothing.

Candace drew the line at Martin purchasing a gun. They'd fought for days over it, mostly over the amount of money it would cost. Martin explained that the musket was the most important element, that the rest of his costume would fall apart without it. She didn't care.

Martin ordered it anyway, spending a chunk of their savings to purchase a Springfield 1855 rifle musket, a rich, dark walnut color.

"You're going to kill yourself with that. Or worse, someone else," she'd told him upon seeing it.

"Don't worry, it's just for looks. It'll shoot blanks." He picked the rifle up. "Pow!" he said, arching the gun back in a mock fire. He aimed it to her. "Pow, pow, pow!"

Even though Candace told him she didn't want to be involved, Martin still decided to buy her an outfit to wear—a Victorian style dress with a hoop skirt and a matching bonnet. Both the bonnet and dress had a white lace trim. Along with these, Martin had purchased a his-and-hers nightgown set. He held up the nightgown to show her. It was all white with gathered cuffed sleeves. It had a light blue drawstring ribbon at the neck, the color matching the stripes on his own pajamas.

Candace wore the nightgown thinking that maybe this was what everything else had been leading up to, that it all had been an elaborate way to liven up their sex life.

"It's itchy," she said after putting it on. "What kind of fabric is this?"

"Should be cotton. That's what I thought at least. The package said 100% authentic."

"Authentically cheap. Can I take it off?" She scratched the back of her neck and the cuffs where the fabric chafed her skin.

"You're not even trying," Martin said, and wanting to give him this at least, she kept it on. She spent the night in the outfit, and in the morning she'd awoken to hives covering her skin—thick scaly blisters that took weeks to finally heal.

Candace took long drives to cope, wasting gas on two-lane stretches of road. A few minutes and she was out of their town, the scenery before her interspersed with corn and soybean fields. The further out she drove, the more desolate it became. Farmland changed to the wide flat expanse of plains. She drove until the sun melted into the horizon, until the needle on the gas dipped close to empty, and then she turned for home.

After her drive, Candace would stop at Clark's to pick up groceries for dinner. She met the kid there at her husband's store. She'd only talked to him once to say thank you when, not paying attention, she'd left her keys on a shelf while looking for a box of cereal. When she'd gone back to get them he was standing there in the aisle, jingling the keys between his fingers.

"I saw you leave them."

"And you didn't think to tell me?"

"I wanted to see how long it'd take you to notice," he said, smiling.

The next week she spotted him across the parking lot waiting at the bus stop. Without his uniform, he looked abandoned and lost. He needed a haircut and to clean his fingernails. Despite all this he was still good-looking, unnervingly so. She wondered if he knew, if he dressed this way in spite of himself, or if he had any idea at all.

Chain smokers puffed out clouds of ash around him. The sun beamed down causing him to squint as he made casual glances down the street for the bus. Candace was making her way to the car when she saw him and asked if he wanted a ride.

Convinced a person does a favor once and they can't not do it again, Candace soon gave him rides whenever she found her way to the grocery. She found she checked often to see if they needed another gallon of milk or if the sugar container was running low, giving another excuse to get in her car and go. His schedule changed from week to week so she was never sure when he'd be there. Some days she missed him and when they happened, she'd wander the aisles trying to appear aimless, like she was merely browsing when deep down she had only one reason for being there.

It was just a one-sided, harmless crush to pass the time, she told herself, and taking him home was an act of goodwill. Neither of them said much in the car and so to fill the silence she often played the radio, turning it to a pop station to sound hip, and each time after she dropped him off she felt foolish and told herself not to get carried away with the thought. At home, Martin acted as if things weren't any different between them. Over dinner he asked about her day, told work stories about his. He helped her clear the table and offered to dry the dishes. It wasn't until afterward—once the dishes were cleaned and put away and they'd exhausted the conversation between them, that Martin left her to go downstairs to their basement to prepare. He told her he needed a space of his own and she hadn't argued about it, but he spent hours reading Civil War history books he'd bought a dime a dozen or watching old films he'd never had the slightest interest in before. Upstairs, she listened to the commotion from the battle scenes from *Glory*, listened as he paused and then rewound certain parts. She tried to picture him down there staring at the screen with a determined hope. Nights she dreamed of bayonets.

An afternoon came when Candace pulled up to his curb and said she couldn't take him home anymore and that this would be the last time.

"Perhaps I never should have started this in the first place. I'm sorry, I hope you understand."

Instead of asking for a reason, or even saying anything at all, he reached over and kissed her. His chapped lips touched hers, his tongue entered her mouth, and it was only when his hands reached for her skirt she told him to stop.

"Look at you," she said. If she'd had a child by now they would have been the same age. If she'd had a girl they might have even dated. "You're a kid. You're so goddamn young and you don't even realize it."

"And you're so goddamn old," he snapped, then his face softened. "I'm sorry. I shouldn't have said that."

Candace sighed. "My husband has decided to become a Civil War reenactor," she said, feeling as though she was unburdening some deeply lodged secret.

"I don't know what that is."

"He dresses up in costumes. Period pieces from the era. Him and a bunch of other men then reenact the war. Pretend like they're really in it."

"Like a play?"

"Sort of, but without an audience. They have them for the major battles, but not always. Depends on the group I guess."

"What's the point then?"

"To fix his middling life, I guess. I don't know, he says it's just a hobby. A game."

"Sounds kind of cool," he said.

"They want to dress up and play around with the past, pretend to change it, but that's all it is—pretend. You can't change what's already happened. Believe me, I know."

Candace didn't tell him but she thought back to the years when her and Martin tried having kids. He'd blamed her for not being able to get pregnant. Worried it was true, she'd gone to three different gynecologists and had herself examined. Each one told her the same thing, that nothing was wrong. She was perfectly capable of having kids.

Martin was infertile. He'd blamed her when the problem was with him.

Candace never told him what she learned. In the beginning she thought it was because she loved him and in the end it didn't matter if they never had children. How could she have known the regret of that decision?

"I wanted a family," Candace said. "It was the only thing I wanted and didn't get. You can't change that."

"What?"

Hearing the kid's voice jolted her from the memory. "Nothing, I should take you home," she said, and he didn't ask again.

Martin made friends from the group he'd joined. One of them was Floyd, a beginner like Martin, and the two of them quickly bonded over their level of inexperience. Weekends, Martin brought Floyd home and the two of them sat hunched over the kitchen table poring over strategies. Floyd was a tall, hunkering sort, with broad shoulders and a thick beard he often rubbed when listening to Martin. Despite his looks, he was soft-spoken, his responses to her often a low murmur she had to ask him to repeat.

Their gatherings had started innocently enough. They met to discuss further what had been talked about in their meetings. They looked through Civil War magazines and brushed up on the history. Most days they weren't even in the house. She peeked through the blinds to watch as they surveyed the suburban landscape around them, the neighboring single-family homes and manicured lawns.

It was Martin's idea to dig the trench, that's what Floyd told her late one afternoon. Martin thought they could better prepare if their environment looked more realistic to what they'd eventually experience. Floyd had come inside from the heat to get a drink of water. When he saw her he immediately apologized for what they were doing.

"Does he have any plans at least? How to go about doing it?"

"No, I don't think so," Floyd said. "I can tell him to stop. Maybe I can change his mind about it."

The kid had complained to Candace about his hours being cut. He thought it was because Martin knew she'd been spending time with him. Candace assured him Martin didn't, he was too pre-occupied to notice, but now she wondered differently. What had become a hobby was increasingly infiltrating her life. She watched as her husband butchered their lawn, knew that soon the neighbors would complain, and couldn't help but think that maybe some of this was being done for spite.

"No, it's all right. "Let him go ahead and dig his hole if he wants it."

"Yes'm," Floyd muttered before walking back out into the sun. The trench would help Martin prepare for his first battle, a reenact-ment of the Battle of Little Blue. Martin wanted her to come, asking her on more than a few occasions, but each time she had told him that she would think about it. It was the best answer she could give, because whenever she thought about the whole thing, the more she hated it, found it stupid and pointless.

"Lots of people come to watch. Spectators. Families are there for support. Friends. You'd be surprised. Not all groups even let people come, some are completely closed events."

"I still don't want to go."

"Why not?"

"Because it's embarrassing," she said flatly. "If you want to know the truth of it."

To Martin it was romantic. He imagined soldiers fighting valiantly, giving up their lives for a cause or purpose greater than them. To him, the war meant honor and courage, sacrifice and survival, but to Candace, the war conjured images of blood—of limbs ripping, bodies being blown to bits. The wild thrashing of the half-dead, their moans numbed out by the sound of ammunition. Broken men, morale wounded from months of pestilence and death. They were starving and dirty. Most of them young, barely eighteen, and had yet to know the world and the beauty it offered—the slight curve of a naked woman's back, the bliss of a satisfied desire. This war was their adventure, for a lot of them the only one they'd ever know, and it was filled with nightmares.

A world not worth reliving, and Candace couldn't imagine why Martin, or anyone, would want to.

As Martin began spending more time preparing for his upcoming battle, Candace spent more time with the kid. Without sex she realized she enjoyed his company, even though mostly all they did was hang out in his apartment while he smoked pot and they both listened to old vinyl records. He cooked her egg sandwiches on a little hotplate. They smoked cigarettes and played cards and she talked about Martin. On a few occasions they went out together. He took her to late-night shows at a movie theater downtown. The theater was frequented mostly with the college kids and she liked it because she knew no one would recognize her. Adjacent to the theater was a video rental shop where the kid would rent movies for them to watch on the evenings when they'd seen everything the theater was playing.

The kid liked to bring her here. The first time she saw it, she understood the place's appeal. Desk-like chairs used for seats filled the screening room. Near the front were a couple of large black sofas where the kid liked to sit.

"You can bring drinks in here too if you want," he plopped down on one. "Just like home."

"What is that, up there?"

She pointed to the corner of the screen where a mechanical robot sat.

"The story is it's a gift from an old employee who had his first job here, went off to become some sort of engineer. He made the thing for a class project or something."

"Does it work?"

"I think so. Should, at least."

The more Candace stared at the robot, the more she wanted it. She couldn't concentrate on the movie or the kid's attempts at holding her hand in the dark. The robot stared back at her, tempting her desire, mocking her misgivings.

After the film ended, once the few others who'd been in the theater left and it was just the two of them watching the credits, she got up from her seat and walked to where the robot was. She reached for it but it was too high.

"You going to help me or what?"

The kid didn't ask or try to convince her otherwise. He hoisted her up and quickly she grabbed it.

"Thanks." Candace took her coat and wrapped it around the robot. She held it close to her chest. "Come on, let's get out of here," she said.

It was late, no one noticed as they walked out of the theater and the cafe. Once outside in the cold night air, she felt exhilarated from her recklessness, in doing something stupid and daring, yet something she wanted. Blood rushed to her face, making her feel alive.

"That was awesome," the kid yelled. They both laughed and he took her arm and pulled her down the street. He pulled her until they both were running. Her face and bare hands stung from the cold but she kept running, following him as far as he'd lead her. They ran down the empty streets, passing closed boutique stores and hair salons and restaurants. They ran until he'd brought her to the back parking lot of an Italian eatery. White Christmas lights decorated the overhang and a few of the surrounding trees.

"Okay, here?" she asked. "Shall we try it here?"

"Yeah," he nodded.

She slid off her coat and handed him the robot. "You do it," she said while putting it back on.

"Fuck. The remote. We forgot it. It's not going to work without it."

"You're kidding me."

"We did all this for nothing. God, I've been so stupid." Candace said, her face flushed.

"I didn't think it was stupid."

"Of course you wouldn't. You're just a college stock boy working at my husband's store. What do you know?"

"Well, what do you want to do now?"

"Nothing. Let's just forget it. I'll take you home."

"I can walk," he said. The kid stared at the robot, as if any moment it would start working. "What should we do about this?"

"I'll deal with it."

"Okay, well, I'm going to go." The kid seemed to say it in a way that was asking her for permission. He needed her to let him go.

Candace watched him disappear. When he was gone she picked herself up from the ground, wiped the dead grass and dirt from her jeans before reaching for the robot. She cradled it in her arms as she walked, the street lights illuminating the robot's metal exterior as she passed them by.

Martin was waiting up for her when she pulled onto the driveway of their house. She'd hoped he'd be asleep by now, usually was, and was surprised to see the gleam of the lights coming out of the window. She parked, turned off the car and got out, carrying the robot along with her. Somehow, it felt heavier than it had before, and she struggled carrying it across the yard. She stopped after a few moments because the metal edge of its body scraped against her hip. She shifted the weight, and afterwards, not paying attention to where she was walking, fell into Martin's trench.

"Damn it," she muttered as she tried to stand. The moment she put weight on her foot a sharp, searing pain went up her leg. She cursed again and sat back down.

Compounding this, it had rained a few days before and the trench was filled with thick mud. It was caked all over her hands and clothes. She thought maybe she could pull herself out, but because of the mud she couldn't grab hold onto anything to support her and instead fell back down again.

Not knowing what else to do she began to yell.

Martin came running. He was dressed in his muslin nightshirt, being too big for him that it came down past his knees. A little matching cap sat on his head with tufts of his hair sprouting from underneath. She saw him and couldn't help but laugh.

"Are you okay? What happened?" Martin said. He started unbuttoning the cuffs from his nightshirt and pulling the sleeves up to his elbows. She watched him as he took this small effort to save his clothes and she laughed harder.

""What's so funny? Why are you laughing?"

"You look ridiculous," she finally said.

"I do? You're the one covered in mud."

Martin leaned down and reached for her. She wrapped both arms around his shoulders and holding on, he pulled her out.

"It hurts to walk. It's my ankle."

"Alright, hold onto me then," Martin told her. Using his support, they both walked to the house.

"Oh, the robot," she said once they were inside. "I left it out there. You need to get it."

Martin gave her a look but nodded and went back inside. He came back carrying the robot she'd left in the ditch. It was streaked with mud and clumps of grass were stuck in some of the crevices. He placed the robot so it was sitting on one of the chairs and then he sat down beside it.

"What are you doing with something like this?"

"I stole it tonight." She didn't bother with the story just told him where it came from and that she'd taken it and it needed to be brought back.

"Why would you do something like that?"

"For the same reason you're doing your civil war shit."

"You still don't understand," he said sighing.

"No Martin, I really don't." Exhausted, depleted, she fell into the sofa. He stood there waiting for her to do something, respond somehow, or at the least answer his question. There was more she wanted to say, like how she felt she didn't know him anymore. They were drifting, had been even before he'd told her about the reenactments. She felt like they were strangers and she didn't know what to do about any of it. She wanted to confess the affair, she wanted to cleanse herself of what had happened. She wanted somehow, to start over, but deep down knew that she never could.

"I just don't know," she finally said.

"I like doing it Candace. I've worked hard my entire life, done everything that was asked, and I enjoy doing this."

"What about the store?"

"That puts a roof over our head. It was my father's, you know that. Not something I really wanted for myself."

"I always thought," she said and then faltered.

"I know there were things you wanted too. I'm sorry they didn't happen, but I love you and I hope you love me enough to understand that this makes me happy. Perhaps it's a small reason but really it's the only one I have."

"No, it's okay. "Candace said. "I'm sorry, I know I've been awful."

Martin smiled. "Here, let me look at your ankle," and he leaned over to look. His hands felt over the skin, rubbing and pressing in different places. "Nothing's broken. Some ice and elevation might do the trick, and if not in the morning I'll take you to the doctor. Until then, maybe it's time we go to bed."

Martin stood and then offered his hand.

"What about the robot?"

"Oh," he said, sighing. "Well, I guess I'll take this back in the morning and apologize."

"You shouldn't have to do that. I was the one that took it."

"We could keep it," Martin paused. "Why not?"

"There's an idea," Candace said, and Martin smiled.

The Battle of Little Blue was minor in the larger context of the war. After a five-hour long stretch the Confederate Army won. It's unclear as to how many soldiers died during it or who most of them even were. For these reasons members of the group chose this battle first to reenact. They liked how it was a battle that could alternate into different scenarios. They liked that they could mettle with the details, have fifty men or five hundred participate.

On this day of the reenactment men congregated on both sides of the farmland below. Candace had gotten there right when it was starting and she hurried to see. Martin had left hours before her to change into his clothes and drive down to the stretch of land where the battle was taking place. By the time she'd woken up, he was already at the camp with the soldiers, going over battle plans and maneuvers for possible outcomes.

A large group of people had gathered on the top of a nearby hill. Mostly women and children, families of the men participating. Candace thought to join them but decided against it, preferring to stay a distance further. On another day perhaps she could handle their conversations but today she just wanted to watch. She searched through hundreds of anonymous faces for her husband, hoped he would see that she came.

These men, they were lawyers and doctors and teachers and mechanics, factory workers and carpenters. They worked farms, tilled soil, managed crops. They had wives, families, children. There were middle-aged men and some looked as young as eighteen.

So many different lives had culminated together for this, to stand underneath the blazing, sun-drenched sky. Hundreds of men sweated under layers of clothes, a heavy musket in one arm, the itchy wool of a cap irritating their skin. They had spent hundreds of dollars and countless hours practicing to make it seem real. None of it was but she felt the thunder of the ground beneath her feet, watched as the men rushed towards each other, many going down within the first few minutes, their bodies colliding with the dirt as others stormed past, and the rush of believing made her breathless. It all became violently and urgently real, and Martin was down there in the thick of it.

More battles would come after this day. They'd replicate others that people remembered. Fort Sumter. Shiloh. Antietam, where more men died than in any other battle in American history. In a few months it'd be the anniversary of Gettysburg, considered to be the turning point, the mark that changed the axis of the war. This battle Candace now watched was just a small one in comparison, holding not much significance in the greater context.

Yet, it was the insignificant—a husband's hobby, a brief kiss, an impulsive act of recklessness—that had avalanched into this. An explosion sounded. Smoke from a cannon clouded over the men. She couldn't see but heard the staccato pop of muskets. Carbine and artillery boomed. A sudden, unexpected longing surged from inside her chest. She stood at the top of the hill, a hand to her throat, watching in hushed breath. It could take hours or minutes for this to be over but she would wait for however long. She wanted her husband to rise from the tumbled mess below. For whatever reason it became important for her to have that, for him to see her standing there waiting, just to have him see, and come back to her okay.

BEANTOWN

by
JENNIFER MORALES
Published in *Acentos*

Candy can't play at my house. I think it's because of the pokey tree in the front yard. One time she came to play and a sharp piece from the pokey tree got stuck in the side of her foot and she cried when her mom came even though my sister pulled it out right after lunch and Candy's mom didn't come get her until *Match Game* came on TV, which is only a little while before dinner. It only bleeded a little bit, but when her mom came she cried and cried. It didn't just happen—it happened a long time before but she was still crying.

That was when we just started K-5 morning class and Candy

doesn't come over anymore. I told my mom we need to cut down the pokey tree and she said *why* and I said *because I want my friend to play at our house.* Mom just stared out the window at the apple tree in the backyard a long time, so I said *that's not the tree Mom,* and I tried to pull her to the front window to show her the one that makes the sharp brown triangles that make your friends can't come over anymore.

We had chorizo and potato tacos for dinner and I picked out all the icky onions because onions are for the birds. My K5 teacher, Miss Monroe, says "for the birds" when she doesn't like something. I don't know what the birds are going to do with all the stuff Miss Monroe and I don't like, but they can have my disgusting onions.

Mom said to my biggest sister, Miriam, "Candy's mom was surprised to find out we are Mexican."

She said this in a boring grownup voice. Grownups talk about boring stuff all the time but when they want me to pay attention they use a different voice, not the boring voice. But I got interested because they were talking about Candy and her mom.

"She was very sorry she sent Candy home on the bus with Elina. She kept calling her Helena. HELL-en-uh."

Mom laughed a laugh that means it's not really funny.

"She said she didn't realize any Mexicans lived on this side of West Avenue." One of Mom's cejas went all the way up to her hair.

I tried to push my ceja up with my finger and show Mom but she made the déjalo face and I let it go.

Miriam said, "Did she say it, like, in a prejudiced way?" Miriam is 17 and likes to use long grownup words she learns at high school.

"What other way could she say something like that?" Mom's mouth made a straight line.

"That's dumb," Miriam said.

Miriam was eating salad because one time she said she doesn't want to get fat like Mom. Mom and Miriam didn't talk to each other for a long time after Miriam said that. I liked when they didn't talk to each other because then I got to be the bringer of messages and I ran through the house so fast to bring the message and nobody yelled at me because nobody yells when you are bringing an important message like tell your sister it's her turn to run the vacuum.

I asked *what does prejutist mean* and Mom said *nothing good* and then she looked at Miriam and her ceja went up again. Then Mom told Patricia and Linda and Karen and Daniel to eat even though they were already eating and she didn't look at my face for all the whole dinner after that.

Sometimes Mom stops looking at us when she is tired because she only has two eyes—she doesn't have eyes in the back of her head, you know—and she has to keep her two eyes on all six kids when my dad is away at the Army and that makes them tired.

• • •

I asked Candy at K5 the next day *are you still my friend even if your mom is a prejetust?* And Candy said *what is that* and I said *nothing good.* And Candy got mad and shouted that I belonged in Beantown and not on Gates Street because Mexicans aren't allowed to live on Gates Street.

I stood up and shouted too. I shouted *I do belong on Gates Street because that is where I live in my little yellow house with the red fence and all my sisters and my brother live there and sometimes my dad too when they let him come home from the Army and my mom.* And then I pushed Candy over and shouted *you know that I live there because that's the place where you got the pokey tree part in your foot and if you didn't cry to your mom like a big stupid baby you could still come over anytime you wanted to.*

This was when we were supposed to be listening quietly to Miss Monroe read the book about Sarah goes to the dentista but we were not quiet. I was crying and Candy was crying and Miss Monroe closed the book and said *girls whatever has gotten into you?* And I pulled my sweater over my head and said *that's stupid, how could anything get into me unless I eated it?* And Miss Monroe said *what, I can't hear you through your sweater.* So I pulled my sweater back down and my hair got full of electric and was waving everywhere and it felt like bugs. I said *how could anything get into me unless I eated it?* And Miss Monroe laughed and said *it's a figure of speech* and I said *why, because I have to figure it out?* And Miss Monroe laughed some more.

She made me sit on the rug by her chair on one side and made Candy sit on the other side. Then she got out the windmill cookies with the canela sugar sprinkles from the special cabinet and every-body got one. I peeked at Candy between the chair legs and she was still crying but not making any noise and mocos were coming out of her nose onto her cookie. I turned my head away because Candy is a big crybaby who eats moccs, but my hair kept reaching for her because of the electric.

• • •

For all the bus rides after that day and all the recess times on the patio, this is what I wondered me: If Mexicans can only live in Beantown and we are Mexican but we live on Gates Street, maybe we are not Mexican? I didn't like this idea one bit because if you are Mexican you get to eat the good food. In your house, you don't have to eat the beans in the can that are light orange and taste like syrup or the smooshy corn that looks like mocos or tuna salad with the green pickles that are bright and shiny like broken glass or Salsaberry steak.

If you are Mexican you can speak Spanish when you don't want the librarian or the doctor or someone working in a store to know that you are telling your parents that they are scary looking or have something icky growing on their face. And even if your parents get mad they will yell at you in Spanish and Doctor Scary-mole-face will not understand.

Also, Mexican dresses are better than American dresses and if you are Mexican and in K5 you can wear a pink dress with 12 ruffles but the American dress only has one or three and socks that match with pink roses on them.

And on your birthday if you are Mexican you get a piñata and you get so many turns even if your big cousins hit it so hard and it breaks a little bit. On your birthday, you get to be the one who hits it the last time and makes the candy fall out.

How could we not be Mexican? I could not understand. I wondered me if there was a circle drawed around Beantown and it had one long part like a paleta stick that reached over just to only our house. Then we would be in Beantown and we would be in the little yellow house too.

I kept looking and looking to see that we are not really Mexican. But at my tía's house in Beantown, her house has the Mexican smell and our house has the Mexican smell. Also, all the families who lived on our street had mostly yellow-haired people and light-brown-haired people. We have all black-haired people, so we are different from all of them. Only Miyuki and her family in the green house on the corner have all black-haired people also. Nobody in K5 plays at Miyuki's house either even though she is not Mexican.

One day, riding in the car with my mom to work at the church, I had another idea: We *are* Mexican but when we cross West Avenue from the side where we live, we get not-Mexican. Like if we are at Mr. Sosa's the barber in Beantown and Dad is getting his hairs cut, we are Mexican, but then when we go to the A&P, where the white people shop and the good sugar cereal comes from, we are not

Mexican anymore, but it's only for a little while, so that's OK.

I holded my hair to see if anything changed when we crossed back over West on the way home from church, but it stayed black the whole time. Also, I spoke Spanish the whole way just in case, but my mouth and tongue feeled exactly the same and then Mom said *basta, Eli,* and she said *cállate* and Daniel said *yeah cállate, parlanchina* and laughed and I knew what they said so we were still Mexican and I wasn't even mad at my brother.

I couldn't decide if I was Mexican at school or not and then one time some kids from grade 4 called me wetback on the patio and I asked my mom what it means and she said *it's a very bad word, don't you say it* and I said *a bad word for being Mexican?* And she said *yes.* And that's how I knew I was Mexican at school.

• • •

The best day in the whole world was dad is coming back day. Miriam and Linda hanged up the papel picado with lovebirds that Mom and Dad got from Mexico when they had their wedding and I wasn't even born yet and Mom made a chocolate cake and Daniel and I drawed a card that said *welcome home Dad.* It really said *welcome home Dad from the stupid Army place* but Mom made us use black crayons and color over the stupid Army part. Miriam tried to make us put some flowers on it like the black part was dirt but Daniel said Dad doesn't like flowers he likes guns. When nobody was watching, Daniel and I drew two Army guys with guns.

When Dad came home we all yelled at him the second he came into the door and we all tried to hug him at the same time and he tried to kiss all of our heads at once but Mom was being greedy with his face. We eated the cake and I sat on his one knee and Daniel sat on the other knee and nobody else got any knees. He said he liked our card very much.

That night was an early to bed night even though it was a Friday and I didn't have to go to K5 in the morning. It was hard to sleep because I was so excited and also because Mom played her Pedro Infante record so loud.

• • •

In the morning, Mom made pancakes and eggs and nopalitos and jamón and Dad said he missed home cooking and squeezed her around the middle like she was a big lemon and he was trying to get all the juice out. Mom laughed and said to Linda *put on Johnny Mathis* and Linda did and Mom sang all the songs until it was time to turn the record over.

After Dad had his nap on the couch and we all washed the dishes so quietly as mouses, Dad waked up and said *I'm going to David's.* I got my shoes on so quick and said *I'm going too* and then Daniel and Pati copied me and Dad said *OK* and it was four people in Dad's car but I got to ride in front.

David's is the store where tortillas come from. There is also other food from Mexico like chiles and tamarindo candy and on

Sunday they have real tamales but on Saturday, Monday, Tuesday, Wednesday, Thursday, and Friday you can only get the icky kinds that come in the jar. David's is the best place to go because there are piñatas and every time I pick one out and my parents say *it's not your birthday yet* and I say *yes it is, it's my birthday when I say it is and I say it is today.* But I only really get one piñata when I have a real birthday and get a new number, like 4 or 5.

In the car, Dad singed a song about going to Beantown. Not a real song, just a song that Linda and Miriam like on the radio that says *bad, bad Leroy Brown*, but he changed the words. Dad singed *bad, bad, bad Beantown, baddest part of the whole damn town.* And I am not supposed to say damn but grownups can say damn.

And this remembered me of Candy and when we shouted at each other in the classroom. And I asked Dad *is Beantown baddest because that's where the Mexicans live?* And Dad stopped the car even though we were not at David's yet and my head banged on the seat. He stopped the car in front of Ben Franklin. Ben Franklin is where the birds live in cages and they peep and are blue and yellow and green and you can't have them because they prefer to live at Ben Franklin.

And Dad said, "Look at me, Elina. Look at me, Eli mia."

I looked at him, even though I don't like it when grownups make me look at their eyes. Their eyes have too much stuff in them.

And Dad said, "Elina, Mexicans can live wherever they want."

"Are we Mexicans?"

Dad laughed. "Of course we are."

"For real, like really, really real?"

"Yes."

"And we can live wherever we want?"

Pati made a blowing noise with her lips in the backseat. "You are such a baby. You don't know anything."

Dad put his big hand on my shoulder and squished it.

"We can live anywhere we want, mi amor. Who told you that we can't?"

And Pati told him about the time Candy's mom said Mexicans don't live on our side of West Avenue.

"Candy's mom is a pree-je-tust," I said.

"She is, is she?" Dad laughed. He said "pree-je-tust" real quiet. Then he said to me, "Eli, you are going to meet some people in life who don't like you, no matter what you do. You can be as nice as can be, never speak an unkind word, go out of your way to help them, and it won't matter one bit if they don't like the color of your skin."

I looked at my arm. "What's wrong with it?"

"Not a thing. There's something wrong with their heads." Dad turned the car back on and said, "Who wants to go to David's?"

• • •

For San Valentín's day, Miss Monroe told us to bring a card for each student in K5 morning class. She gave us a pink paper with purple letters on it which was the names of our whole class. Miss

Monroe said *We don't play favorites in kindergarten*, so *be sure to bring a card for each person on the list.*

At Alton Drugs, Mom helped me pick out valentines. Mom helps by saying *you can either choose this or this or this*, even though there are one hundred kinds. One of the boxes was dogs and cats and one was balloons and monkeys wearing people clothes. But the other one was rainbow glitter hearts that weren't just cards, they were pockets and in the pocket YOU PUT CANDY.

I said *Mom you put candy in the little pocket and that is a very good valentine don't you think?* Mom said *but then that's one more thing you have to buy* and that is something a mom says right before she says *no we don't have money for that mi amor* and even though she calls you *mi amor* it still means *no* even if you say *but if you love me, you should get me this thing.*

But Mom was a big surprise! She did not say *no we don't have money for that mi amor*. No, her face got pink and her eyes got small and she breathed noisy breaths into her nose like she was going to laugh.

Then she smiled and I didn't know what was going on so I smiled too and she said *it's a special holiday and we should celebrate, right? But we will go to David's to buy the candy.*

I could not believe my very good luck.

At David's, I picked out the little candy hearts that say CALL ME and BE MINE and look like chalk but Mom said *no because we would have to open the box to put hearts in each valentine and they could fall out and get dirty.* I needed to pick a candy with a wrapper, she said, *so they will stay clean.*

I looked and looked and looked. Some things were too spicy and some things were too big to fit in the pocket and some things cost too much money for a whole giant class of 23. When Mom started to say that I needed to choose already, that she needed to go home and cook dinner, I just grabbed a bag of watermelon candies. I do not prefer watermelon, but the wrappers were pink and on Valentine's Day everything pink or red is good.

I spended the time after dinner writing names on my valentines and putting the candy in the pockets. I was so excited to bring the best valentines in all of K5 morning class. I wrote the names very nicely, even the name of Candy who was not my friend. I was very proud.

Mom said to leave the envelopes open so she could check my spelling and she would close them for me, which was good because I don't like to lick those icky sobres that taste like licking the sidewalk. I only licked the sidewalk one time and it was disgusting.

After making the valentines I had to take a bath and Linda had to wash my hair and that makes nobody happy. Even though after a bath I am supposed to get Miriam to dry my hair for me so that I don't die of la gripa, I sneaked downstairs quiet as mouses because I wanted to see if Mom thinked my writing was all good.

Mom was still at the kitchen table and all the sobres were still open and the candies were all took out of the valentines. I opened my mouth to say *Mom what is happening* but then I saw Miriam looking at me from by the sink and her face was like the moon with big wide eyes that said *don't say anything* but not with words.

Mom had the pink paper from Miss Monroe with all the purple names on it and she was reading each one very quiet then finding the valentine that matched.

"Lupe," she said. And she put the candy back into the pocket and licked the icky envelope. I know I writed LUPE very nicely so why she took his candy away in the first place I did not know.

"Alonzo," she said. She looked up at Miriam and said, "Alonzo with a z is Italian, no? If he was Mexican it would probably be an s."

Miriam's mouth opened and closed like Simon, the goldfish in the K5 room, but no sounds comed out. Then she looked at me and did a little dance like she got one hundred and thirty-two spiders on her.

"Probably not Mexican," Mom said.

Then Mom did a terrible thing. She opened the candy and put it in her mouth. Then took it out and put it back in the pink wrapper. She put the candy in the valentine and closed the envelope.

"Un sabor de México," she said. She looked up at Miriam again and did the laugh where it's not funny.

I told my feet to step into the kitchen and grab the rest of the candies but my feet are very naughty and they went the other way, back into the dark hallway.

I watched while Mom read all the names and said if they were Mexican or not. For Magdalena and José and Miguel she put the candies back without putting them in her mouth first. But for everybody else she took them out and licked them all over.

And when she said Candy's name, that one she kept in her mouth for a long, long time.

"A special candy for Candy," she said and this time her laugh said *this is funny.*

I ran upstairs then and put my wet head under my pillow and cried.

• • •

All the way to school on the bus I tried to think what to do. The valentines were in a paper lunch bag in my mochila and they were terrible now. Not one bit fun. Not the best valentines in all of K5.

When the bus stopped in front of the school I waited until Bus Driver Marcie said *are you getting off or what?* and *come on, dear.* She patted my head and I almost told her the terrible news but went down the stairs and into the school.

Right at the start of the day, Miss Monroe said *let's put our valentines on the snack table, friends, and then we will hang our school bags on our hooks,* so I had to take the bag with my terrible valentines out and put it with all the other kids' valentines. My hands were shaking shaking and Miss Monroe said *yes, we're very excited about Valentine's Day, aren't we, Elina?*

Then we made pink paper hearts for our parents and Miss Monroe wrote the letters for I LOVE YOU on the chalkboard for copying and my writer hand was shaking shaking and Miss Monroe comed over.

Are you alright, Elina? she asked me. She made the face of two lines up and down over her nose and that is the face of when you are about to be sent to the nurse. For only one second I thinked *I can go to the nurse and get away* but I was not sick and that is a kind of lying and lying is bad. For another second I thinked *I can tell Miss Monroe to throw away the candy.* Then she would ask me why and I would have to say *Mom licked all the candies* or I would have to say a lie. But we don't lick other people's food so I started to say *Miss Monroe, the candies in my valentines have* and I was going to say *poison* but I stopped. What was worst? Licking or poison?

I thinked of sitting in Mom's big lap after school. Today when I am going to sit in her lap she will ask me if I gave all the valentines to the children.

"Have what, dear?"

I looked at Miss Monroe and I said, *Nothing. But you know, kids in K5 are for the birds.*

THERE'S
THE INDIAN!

---

by
RUBY HANSEN MURRAY
Published in *The Massachusetts Review*

Patrick Xhuda drove his pickup toward the Ranch Wife Restaurant with his Osage clothes hanging in the back seat. Outside of Red Hawk, two cars waited at the drive-through for cigarettes at Strike Axe Trading Post. He had been eating breakfast at home in Hominy, scrolling through his phone, thinking of all the grading he had left to do before the end of school, when he read an ad from the Chamber of Commerce announcing that the Ranch Wife was taking over Red Hawk on July 4th.

"Well, shit," he said.

His wife lowered *The BigHeart Times*. "What?"

"The Campbell woman," he said, pushing the cantaloupe away. Bonnie Campbell, a socialite from the next town, had fashioned herself into a celebrity Ranch Wife on the Internet and the cooking channel. Her new restaurant drew six thousand people, doubling Red Hawk's population, daily. She treated Red Hawk like it was her own theme park. She'd been trying to buy the Montauban Apartments on Main for a luxury hotel. Patrick believed in economic development, but the area needed affordable housing, too.

Jeanne was quiet, tired of what she called Patrick's obsession. His family had history with the Campbells. The old man had been Patrick's grandfather's guardian in the twenties, and a lot of Osage money, a lot of his family's money, had disappeared into Campbell's coffers. She watched as Patrick took his Osage clothes from the cedar chest. He folded his leggings and breechcloth, then placed a ribbon shirt on a hanger and told Jeanne he planned to have lunch at the Ranch Wife Restaurant.

"Why do you need your clothes?" she asked.

"I'm going to wear them," he said, as if that answered anything. "I'll be back mid-afternoon, I guess." Visitors waited in the sun for hours. He didn't know how long he'd be. Patrick aimed a kiss at Jeanne and was at the front door when she told him to wait. She came back holding a water bottle.

"I'm just going to have lunch," he said, but he was already wondering how his back was going to tolerate standing all day. "You can come."

"Why would I want to do that? Besides, the War Mothers are meeting." She stood on the porch of their small house and called, "Don't forget you're working Monday."

Traffic picked up when Patrick turned from the highway onto Main Street at the new Dollar General and Sonic. A pump jack stood idle above an oil well waiting to be capped, one of hundreds across the reservation. Patrick blew a loud breath. His brother had been elected to the Nation's congress on a platform of economic development. It was time for Joe to create the Osage businesses that would clean up the messes the producers had left.

Parked cars lined both sides of Main beginning at Lynn. Outside Hank's Pawn, Skeeter Lapi^kae shut the door on his old Ford pickup and waved. Patrick acknowledged him, wondering if he'd seen the ribbon shirt in the back window. Skeeter, the head committeeman for the Hominy I'n lon schka, would want to know why Patrick was carrying his Osage clothes. Skeeter was old school; he said, "Add nothing, take nothing away" from the dances, the traditions.

A warning rang in Patrick's head, and he considered turning toward home. Of course, he could eat at Bonnie Campbell's in his regular clothes, but that would accomplish nothing. In the parking lot of a shuttered store, an old black man was selling honey from his truck. Patrick braked hard for a trim white woman in her fifties who stepped out in front of him. She paused then gave a little wave. Since the restaurant opened, tourists stood in the middle of Main Street taking photos, oblivious to cattle trucks bearing down on them.

The restaurant occupied the center of downtown at the intersection of Main Street and Osage as it angled north to the agency. The Ranch Wife persona was built on images of pioneer wholesomeness. Her blog featured photos of cowboys feeding snow-dusted Black Angus cattle at dawn on the open prairies west of Red Hawk. Images of horses lining the horizon at sunset and men in Stetsons cycled on screens throughout the restaurant. Self-deprecating posts described life on a working cattle ranch in the middle of nowhere. The Campbells were the fifth largest landowner in the US, and owned more than half of the reservation. Many Osages would never eat at a Campbell establishment, though some slipped in when the lines weren't long.

Patrick set his jaw and inched along Main approaching the corner with Osage Street where the line wrapped around the Ranch Wife's building. He turned right onto Sixth and parked in the shade of the marble-clad Kennedy Bank Building. He opened the passenger doors to form a dressing area. Near the arbors during the I'n lon schka, people from visiting districts or those hurrying after work dressed beside their cars, but no one else was dressing today.

Patrick removed his shirt and pulled on buckskin leggings over his baggiest shorts. He felt foolish, but he added breechcloth, tail, and the hand-woven streamers that his niece made. He laced the bells on his calves. He'd brought a bright pink cotton shirt with green satin ribbons, and he settled his armbands. He touched the fur of his otter hide and prayed that old Uncle Patrick would approve of what he was doing. As he looped the bandolier over each shoulder, he wished he were dressing for a war party, ready to drive the Campbells off the reservation like they should have in the old days.

He folded a white handkerchief and tied it across his forehead. Next, he knotted a leather thong under his chin to keep his porcupine roach tight and set the eagle feather, ducking to see that it was straight. He took a water bottle, another bandana, the keys and his phone in a small leather satchel. He automatically reached for the striped blanket he would have carried to the wooden bench under the arbor, but stopped himself.

The pavement was hot as he started back toward Osage Street in light blue beaded moccasins, and as he walked the bells filled his path. He felt the Hominy men beside him. People near the restaurant turned when they heard him. He walked with the ching ching of his bells into the canned country music that filled Osage Street now. After a long moment, the people started taking pictures as if he were a celebrity. He stood taller, his gut loosening against the wide leather belt.

The hostess, a young woman in shorts and a T-shirt, turned. She was a teenager he'd taught at Red Hawk High School, Crystal Campbell.

"Mr. Xhuda?" she called as he got closer, but he didn't stop.

"Sir?" she said, skipping to catch up. "May I help you? Are you looking for someone?"

"I'm getting in line," he said, as people nudged each other.

"Are you meeting someone? I mean, for photos?" Her cheeks were bright pink in the heat.

"No," he said.

Someone driving by yelled, "Hey, Chief." The windows in the Triangle Building gaped. Marble stairs led to empty offices, foul from years of theft.

When he reached Main at 10:30, it felt like noon. His legs slid against the leggings. Everyone moved slowly, swimming through the humidity. People became quiet when they heard the bells. The porcupine roach and its eagle feather made him a foot taller than he already was. He was carrying his eagle feather fan, because it didn't feel right to leave it. He got in line behind a group of women in their fifties wearing matching OU shirts.

A child shouted, "Indians!" His mouth was cottony; the bells tinkled when he shifted. A hefty white-haired man behind Patrick told his wife the wait was at least three hours.

"I hope it's worth it," said the man, who wore a shirt stenciled with an Open Road RV.

"Is there an event?" his wife asked Patrick. She had a matching Winnebago shirt, short honey-colored hair and a frank, open face.

"No," he said, stretching to loosen the tightness in his back. People who passed took photos, which hit social media by about 10:45. The Winnebago couple's granddaughter held out her phone. Patrick was a big man like his grandfather. He looked serious in the picture, glum actually, which was how he often looked, even though he told good jokes. The caption read, "How cool is this?" @winnebagotraveler #ranchwiferestaurant #CowboysandRealIndians.

"Your clothes are amazing," the granddaughter, a young teenager, said. She was sweating, her face a bright red. "I've never been to a pow wow. Never seen how beautiful the work is." She reached for the woven streamers' row of arrowheads, the weave tight like pebbles side by side.

He stepped back and said, "Don't."

"No need to be sharp," her grandfather said. Patrick's eyebrows rose, but he lifted the fan and moved air across his face. He knew it was ridiculous to have worn his clothes here.

A car pulled up and honked, and his boys got out. "Dad!" Buddy said. He was the youngest with a soft belly in a white T-shirt.

Junior, an inch taller than his Dad, took his father's hand and gave him a half-hug. They acted like he often wore his Osage clothes downtown.

"Didn't have time to dress," Buddy said, clapping Patrick on the shoulder.

"You should have told us." One Indian, even wearing his Osage clothes, was one thing, but seeing four big Indian men, the people began to squeeze into themselves, making room.

"What are you all doing here? Did your mother send you?"

Joseph, the middle brother, said, "Nah, she told us you were here, and we decided to come down." Patrick knew they weren't just hanging out together. Joseph was in summer session in nursing school in OKC, Buddy worked in Tulsa, and Junior managed the casino north of town. Buddy held out his phone. "See?"

Patrick was a blob of bright pink shirt, the headband bright against his forehead. Buddy's feed read #osageinvasion #Wahzhazhis Rule #Wahzhazhi_live_ here_too #osages_overeignty.

"Hope there's enough food left by the time you all get inside." One of the taller OU women had turned around. "These must be your boys. I'm Selma." She extended a hand, and Junior, the most outgoing, took it. A cluster of introductions ensued. The women belonged to the book club of a professional women's sorority. They loved Sherman Alexie; they'd read Linda Hogan, all of Charles Frazier and David Grann.

"Then you know about the Osage Murders," Joseph said. He happened to be wearing a Hominy Bucks purple T-shirt, PRIDE spelled within the sketch of an arrowhead. "Besides the murders, the guardians and lawyers stole so much from us. You know they were in that building right up there." He pointed to the red brick Triangle Building, where shredded plastic flapped from the windows on the fourth and fifth floors.

"They're remodeling, maybe they'll give tours," Buddy said.

"The Ranch Wife's in-laws were a big part of that," Joseph said. "Still are. You know one's running for the Legislature." The women were quiet. "He still has a lawsuit against the tribe."

"Really?" another soror said.

"Here's the Indian," a young woman in a yellow sundress shouted as she came over to ask for a photo.

"You know what tribe is he?" Junior asked.

"He's from around here, right?" she said, flipping long brown hair over a bare shoulder. "Osoggy?"

"It's O-sāge, but yeah. This is our land."

"In the town of Red Hawk?" she said.

"Yeah, it's on the Osage Indian reservation, established in 1877."

"You guys all teachers?" the Winnebago man asked.

"Proud of my boys," Patrick said.

"Hey!" People shouted and clapped in the line ahead. Patrick expected to see the Ranch Wife, but Mary and Andie Walker from Hominy came forward in their Osage clothes. Mary's purple lace shirt shimmered over blue broadcloth. A tall woman, Mary carried her shawl and smiled. Andie walked beside her, looking down her nose like her Dad always did, her mouth in a half smile. They'd seen Patrick on social media, and they understood what he wanted to do.

Watching them coming was like being lifted by helium.

"Hey, Mary," the boys called. "Come eat with Dad." Buddy asked the Winnebago couple if they would mind. There was a chorus of encouragement.

"No, we're going to the back," Mary said. "I bet some of those folks need to hear some Wah Zha Zhi ie."

"Is this Native American day?" the Winnebago man asked. "You all get a discount?"

Mary leaned toward him, her eyes level with his. "Every day is Osage day, dude. We live here." She was strong like an Osage woman, but laid back. People rustled in the line ahead. The Ranch Wife was coming toward them, smiling and posing for photos. She stepped up too close to Patrick and barely said hello before she said, "This is our business. You can't sell anything here."

"We're here for lunch," Buddy said.

The Ranch Wife was wearing jeans tucked into tall cowboy boots with cutouts of the Campbell family brand. Her long blonde hair was braided off her face. The Winnebago granddaughter was filming with her cell phone, moving around her grandfather to get closer.

Bonnie Campbell shaded her eyes, and said, "Well, why don't you come on inside?"

"We'll wait like everyone else," Buddy said.

"We don't want a disturbance," she said. Everyone looked at her, then back at the man in Indian clothes and the three square-built young men in T-shirts and shorts. The sorority women seemed surprised.

Mr. Winnebago said, "They're just waiting. We were talking."

She stood for a moment appraising Patrick before she continued down the line.

"Do we really want to eat here," Joseph asked. The granddaughter's video caught it all, Joseph's quiet question, Patrick saying, "Sure as hell."

During high school, Patrick would drive his grandmother to Campbell's General Store in Hominy. Old Angus Campbell would come out from the back office to greet her. Gladys would say Haweh and listen to his bumbling Osage. She was fifteen in 1907, when oil money began to flow to each tribal member. Angus Campbell was a trader, licensed after he'd failed in the cattle business. He told the Osage how much he respected them and he told the whites how he'd built his fortune off the Osages.

His grandmother walked with a cane and wore opaque stockings in solid black shoes. She would browse through the store before she ordered what she wanted at the long oak counter. While they drove home, she told Patrick the Campbells didn't know enough to be embarrassed by their greed. She'd curl her fingers into claws leafing through bills. "We called old lady Campbell 'Let-me-count-it-for-you.' They were waxpáoi." She looked to make sure he understood. "Pitiful."

They waited another half-hour. Osages drove by and waved.

Rose Burke, the assistant chief, crossed the street to say hello. A handsome woman with long hair and a wide smile, she lived on a ranch west of town. She stood in a T-shirt and shorts, squinting at Patrick, waiting for him to explain. Finally, she said, "Just having lunch, huh?" and went into a clothing store behind them.

When the sorority sisters entered the restaurant, Junior said, "Dad, are you going to sit inside and eat?" The other brothers looked somewhere other than Patrick. Once when an out-of-town Osage came to their camp still dressed from the evening session and tried to eat without changing first, and their father had set him straight.

Patrick knew this was his last chance to turn around. He felt stubbornness rise: it was time for Osages to stand together. Everyone knew Patrick honored the traditions, and they knew how he felt about the Campbells. Replacing the Montauban with a hotel would put World War II Osage vets Henry Rowland and Sonny Maka out of the apartments they'd occupied for years. When the Nation had built senior housing on the hill, the old men said they liked where they lived. Moreover, Sonny said, the duplexes were too much for one person to care for, and he did not want caregivers looking in on him.

Patrick believed it was better to ask for pardon than permission in his dealings with both the I'n lon schka committee and with the school administration. He was following in the path of his relatives, who changed protocol when they needed to make a new way. Junior's ink black eyes were steady on his face.

"Howeh," Patrick said, just as the young Campbell hostess called them in. Junior put a hand on his father's back, and they stepped inside.

The two-story building had begun as a store for the Osages. The remodel had taken the walls to brick and added a coffee bar and an industrial kitchen. A wall lined with banquettes divided the restaurant from the store.

"How are you all?" Charlene Blue, an Osage who graduated with Buddy, smiled as she held menus. Gleaming black hair hung to her shoulders. If she thought it was unusual to see an Osage dressed to dance, it didn't show.

"I didn't know you worked here," Junior said, while Patrick grinned as he did whenever he saw young Osages.

"There are a few of us," she said.

Charlene led them to a table near the front windows. Patrick walked his soft-soled moccasins across the tiled floor, the bells almost lost in the space. Middle-aged diners of varied shapes and sizes gestured toward him.

When she reached a square table for four, Charlene touched a bentwood chair, raised her perfectly formed eyebrows and said, "Will this be okay, Uncle?"

"Just fine," he said, arranging the otter tail and breechcloth discreetly to the side. Patrick's legs splayed out as he perched on the edge of the chair.

"Would you mind—" Charlene glanced at the hostess stand

and passed her phone to Junior. She leaned close to Patrick, who held his head high, while Buddy scrunched close on other side.

Patrick loosened the leather thong and removed the roach and the eagle feather, and rested them on his thigh. He untied the white handkerchief and wiped his face. They had all laughed at the California Osage who thought he could eat at their camp dressed. He pictured explaining himself to Skeeter, the lines around the older man's mouth.

The waiters wore red and white checked shirts. Their server, a young woman from Copan, took their drink order. She returned with quart jars of iced tea, chirping friendly banter and studiously avoiding Patrick. Across the aisle, the Winnebago family, now seated, smiled and raised Mason jars of soda.

While his sons studied the menu, Patrick considered the old Primrose Flour Mill mural placed above the espresso bar, and the stylized Campbell Ranch brand set into the brick near the kitchen. In the 1950s, Patrick's father had shopped for school clothes here. After the department store had closed, a five and dime filled the space. Patrick and his Red Hawk cousins rode their bikes downtown the summers he stayed with them.

On the store side of the restaurant, customers perused china cups stacked on round tables while oil tankers rumbled by. Cashiers hurried to serve shoppers with baskets full of Campbell Ranch T-shirts and Red Willow dinnerware. Patrick recognized Sylvia Good Eagle checking a customer out.

"Dad—" Buddy said. The woman from Copan waited for his order.

"I'm not very hungry," he said, ordering a sandwich rather than French onion soup that could drip on his vest. The server returned with plates loaded with lasagna, brown gravy over chicken fried steak and rib eye steak. Patrick began to pray, "In da tse Wah kon tah, Wah kon tah I shinke—" the Winnebagoes' granddaughter still filming.

EN PLENA VISTA

by
MICHAEL PACHECO
Published in *Latinx Journal*

Shortly after sunrise, HQ called Special Agent Varela and told him they had detected two homing-device signals. Two cartel trucks had stopped near the Mexican border—all signs pointed to a drop site at a small farm. After pulling up information about the property and its owners, Varela and his men set out to investigate. He felt a lightness in his chest. The Agency had been after these men for a long time.

Varela and his men drove to the location, pulled into a blacktop driveway, and screeched to a halt. A senior couple sat on the front porch of a weathered farmhouse, luxuriating in the mid-morning sun, silently watching the G-men.

The four agents climbed out of their cars and up the porch stairs. Varela reached into his jacket and pulled out a black leather wallet. He thrust it toward the old man, displaying a shiny gold badge.

"Mornin'. Pete Varela, DEA. Are you Barney O'Brien?"

The old man glanced at the badge, then at two of the men in suits as they broke off toward the side of his residence. He didn't appear to be afraid. Varela guessed he'd probably seen lots of testosterone-filled men, carrying weapons out here in the desert, especially the gun-crazed vigilantes.

Those poor immigrant souls, dying of thirst in the hot Arizona desert, rarely made it as far as this farm. Out here, even the Yaqui Indians didn't tread. Their magic was no match for the unforgiving rays of the sun.

"That's me, all right. What are you here for?"

Varela put away his ID and gave a nod to his colleague, who remained at the foot of the porch steps. The agent relaxed at Varela's gesture.

"Well sir," Varela said, "we received word you have two rigs on your property, trailers with suspicious cargo in them."

Barney grinned. "You mean like illegal drugs?"

The old lady reached and covered the man's hand with hers and shrugged. "Might as well tell him."

Varela perked up. "Tell me what?"

Something like a sparkle of joy came over Barney's face. "This here's my wife, Maggie. You got a few minutes? There's a little tale that goes with my explanation 'bout them trailers."

Varela nodded in acknowledgement.

"By the way," Barney said, "your boys can check out the trailers." He waved toward an old wooden structure. "They're parked behind the barn, over yonder."

Varela pointed two fingers at his men and then at the barn like a swat team leader signaling instructions to his men. The men in blue hurried off.

"So, what can you tell me?" Varela asked.

Maggie rose from her wicker chair "Why don't you sit here, Mr. Varela? I'll get us some fresh coffee."

"Thank you, ma'am," Varela said, sliding into the chair. He loved coffee. In fact, his doctor had advised him to cut back on his intake. The caffeine and stress of the job were not good for him. "But I just had a cup at the office," he said. "Besides, I'm just here to get some quick information."

Barney smiled. "I've been expecting you for a while now. Surprised you took this long to get here."

Varela nodded, accepting Barney's point. "We know the trucks and trailers arrived here yesterday, but when the trucks left, we didn't know right away that the trailers were still here. Our undercover agents only attached the tracking devices to the trailers."

"I see," Barney said. He reclined in his chair and clasped his hands on his paunch. "So, now that you found them trailers, is that all you want?"

"You said you had a little tale to tell. Let's hear it," Varela said. "After that, I have a few questions for you."

"Such as?"

"Such as, the model and make of the trucks. You must have seen some markings."

The farmer didn't show any reaction, leaving Varela to wonder if this man still remembered what he did only a day ago.

Before Barney could respond, Maggie appeared with a fresh cup of coffee for him. She glanced at the agent at the foot of the steps, as if to offer him a cup as well, but he simply shook his head.

Barney took the cup and looked at Varela. "You said you were here about them two trailers."

Varela narrowed his eyes. "The Agency believes you have information about the trailers we should know about."

The old man sipped his fresh coffee and grinned. "I was sitting here minding my own business." He pointed to his barn. "When these two trucks pulled up with trailers hitched to 'em."

Varela drew a small notepad from his side pocket and took notes. "You're saying they simply appeared out of the blue? Who drove the trucks? Were they Mexican men?"

Barney shrugged. "Beats me. I figured they were lost. But one guy was dark as night and the other was white as death." He chuckled. "I guessed they were circus people, cause there was clowns painted on the side of the trailers, so it is."

"Did you talk to the drivers?"

Barney grinned. "Well, they spoke English, but we weren't having a normal conversation."

"What do you mean?"

Barney looked out over his acreage, and Varela followed his gaze. The old man's tractor had a flat tire and the hydraulic system for the disk and plow leaked fluid. Weeds covered his farm.

Barney shook his head. "I been short on cash for the past several months, so when those trucks pulled up, I thought, oh dang, traveling salesmen."

"If you had no money, why would you worry about it?"

Barney shook his head. "It wasn't so much worrying as it was the hassle of listening to another sales pitch."

"What were they selling?"

Barney sipped his coffee again as Maggie scooted another chair next to him. He nodded, approving the taste of the hot brew. "Weren't sellin', they were buying."

Varela straightened up at the mention of a purchase. "What were they buying?"

"More like renting. The white guy pulled out ten hundred-dollar bills outta his pocket and handed them to me," Barney said. "'This money is yours,' he says, 'if we can park our trailers here for a spell, let's say a day or two.' Well sure, that's a grand arrangement, says I, and I took the money, and they was gone."

"Didn't you ask what was inside the trailers?"

"Nope, why would I? There was nothing leaking from them, you know, like oil or something."

Varela jotted more notes. He glanced up as his colleagues waved at him from the barn. They appeared intrigued by something, but Varela wanted to hear the old man out, so he raised his hand in acknowledgment and shifted his focus back to Barney.

"Didn't it seem odd to you that a stranger would offer you a thousand dollars for parking a couple of trailers on your property? Not a smart move, Mr. O'Brien. You may have committed a crime by harboring contraband."

"Eventually, yes. I knew they weren't being candid with me," he said, looking down, "but all I saw was the money."

Varela looked up from his notepad. "What tipped you off about them not being honest?"

"Well, right before they left, I asked them what their names were."

The agent readied his pen. "And?"

"And the dark-skinned guy said his name was Asada. I figured he might be a foreigner."

"Hmmm. Muslim?"

"But nothing nasty. If that's what you're thinking. In fact, he was downright friendly. Both of them were."

"What was it about the name that concerned you, then?"

Barney glanced at Maggie and grinned. "It was Maggie that opened my eyes to it."

"Opened your eyes to what?"

"As they turned to leave, the white guy handed me the money and said, 'You can call me Carney.'"

Varela stopped writing. The corners of his mouth turned upward. "Right. Carney Asada."

"Yup, me and Maggie had a good laugh, but we had a thousand dollars, too."

"And the trailers?"

Barney looked at his wife and grinned. "Well, that there's a whole different story."

"Hold on," Varela said as he reached into his right-side pocket. He pulled out a recorder and pushed a button. He set it on the wicker table. "Okay, continue."

Barney frowned at the contraption. "That's a strange-looking yoke. What is it?"

"It's called an iPhone," Varela said, "but I'm connected to my office and the recording is taking place there."

Barney looked at his wife once more, smiled, and then shrugged. "Okay, but sometimes those things don't work out here."

"You mean like poor reception?"

"I mean like *disappearing* reception. Sometimes they work, and sometimes they don't."

Varela turned and glanced at his colleague behind him. The agent shrugged. "I'm not sure I know what you're referring to, but my phone is working fine."

"Suit yourself," Barney said. He took a big swig of his coffee and then set down his cup. He leaned back in his chair and locked his hands together. "So, about those trailers. How strange."

"How's that?"

"It's funny. That same day the men left the trucks here, we were frettin' over losing our farm."

"What was strange about that?"

"That's not the strange part," Maggie said. She tapped the back of Barney's hand. "Tell him, Honey."

"I'm getting there, I'm getting there." Barney downed the rest of his coffee. "Like I said, I took a gander at the trailers after the drivers left. Maybe I was still a little curious about getting free money for these trailers just sittin' on my property. Anyway, I was getting ready to come back to the house when I heard a banging noise comin' from inside the trailers."

"Both of them? You mean like a person banging or a metallic banging or what?"

"It was a hard banging, kinda like a person slapping the side of the trailer wall."

Varela picked up his phone and inspected it. The signal was gone. This was unusual. It was working just a minute ago. He stood and walked a few paces to another spot. Still nothing. He set it down again, then decided he'd have to take more copious notes. "So, what did you do?"

"I yelled at the trailer doors. I figured if it was a person in there, they'd yell back at me."

Varela looked up from his notepad. "What did you yell and did someone respond?"

"Sorta. I said, 'Quien esta?' Then I heard a banging sound from both of the trailers, like someone trying to get out."

"What did you do?"

"Maggie and I figured it might be people in there, you know, illegals. We heard those coyotes just let people die out here. After a minute, all the banging just stopped."

Varela felt like a fish on the hook. He always wanted to see the best in people, but he didn't trust anyone's word without proof.

Barney glanced at Maggie. "How many cups of coffee have I had today?"

"Only two," she said.

Varela shifted in his seat. "Mr. O'Brien?"

"Yes?"

Varela's frustration and irritation were both rising fast. "Did you let them out?"

"Let who out?" Barney must have seen the anger bubbling up in Varela. "Okay, okay, I'm just coddling ya. Yeah, I opened the door on the first trailer."

He handed his empty cup to Maggie, who then went back inside the house. "On the first truck, I unlocked the hatch, opened the door and there it was."

Varela looked up from his notepad. "What exactly was there?"

"It was a huge cow lying on its side. Looked dead to me, probably bloated from the heat." He smiled at Varela. "It was over 115 degrees yesterday."

Varela tapped the pen on his pad several times, then set it down. He took a deep breath, forcing himself to stay calm. "Mr. O'Brien, we're not here to harass you, so you need to be serious about this. This investigation has been ongoing for quite some time."

"Oh no, Mr. Varela," Maggie said. "We wouldn't lie about something like this."

"I suppose the sounds you heard were the cows kicking the door?" Varela said, trying to hold back the sarcasm in his voice. When neither Barney nor Maggie smiled at his joke, he followed up with another question. "So, when are the truck drivers coming back for the trailers?"

"Well, I don't really know, a couple days?"

Varela sighed and looked at Mrs. O'Brien. "Thank you all for your time."

Barney nodded. "Sorry you didn't find that suspicious cargo you were looking for."

Varela shook his head in disbelief. These Irish *viejitos* were lying through their false teeth or going senile. He rose and glared at O'Brien.

"One way or another, I'm gonna find out what really happened here."

He climbed down the stairs. "Come on," he said to his colleague, and then stomped to where the other agents waited. "What the hell did you find out there?"

One man shrugged. "Not much. Footprints of a couple men and a couple dead cows, one in each trailer."

Just then a dust-devil danced near the trailers. Something within it glittered in the sun, and within seconds, it dissipated into thin air.

Varela stared at the agent for a second, then gazed out across O'Brien's fallow land. He ran his hand through his hair. What on God's green earth was going on out here?

Upon their return to the field office, Varela reported back to his supervisor. "Dead end," he said. "Actually, dead cows is more like it. They were on their side, mouths open, probably heat stress. I'm guessing we fell for a classic distraction maneuver by the coyotes. We went to the O'Brien farm while they transported their wares somewhere else."

The supervisor stared at him. "Just cows?"

"That's all we found," Varela said, wondering whether he'd missed something.

His boss opened a bottle of water and took a swig, then looked Varela. "Some agents, when looking for proof of criminality, see things that don't exist while blind to the evidence right before their eyes. You're not one of those agents, are you, Varela?" Then, before Varela could answer, the supervisor said, "What did the cows look like?"

His supervisor stared at him the way his father used to when he was little and working out a puzzle. Daddy wouldn't give him the answer. He'd let Varela solve it on his own. And then it dawned upon him. The smuggled drugs were stashed inside the cows and probably had killed them too.

"Oh, shit!" Varela said. "I'm on it, boss." He waved an agent toward him and rushed out the door.

At the O'Brien farm, he went to the main house door and knocked. While waiting for someone to answer, he scanned the farmyard, searching for the trailers. They were gone.

Barney answered the door. "Back so soon?"

"Hello, Mr. O'Brien. We need to see those trailers again."

"Too late for that."

"Where are they?"

"Those same men came by and picked them up, right after you left."

Varela let out a deep sigh. "I told you to call me, if anything happened with those trailers."

"I did, but like I said, there's no reception out here. Oh, by the way, they told me to give these to you." He turned and reached behind him. When he faced Varela again, he handed him the two homing devices.

<hr>

BEER &
BUTTER SAUCE

<hr>

by
TISHA MARIE REICHLE-AGUILERA
Published in *New Delta Review*

"Take this to Gramps. Careful. It's hot." Granny wraps the green and gray hot pad around the broken handle and hands me the tiny silver pot. 'And don't go drinking it. I know how much you love butter." She cackles and turns her attention to the biscuit dough.

"I won't drink it." I stop in the doorway. "All the beer's burned off now."

Granny clicks her throat and flicks some of the sticky dough from her fingertips at me.

I kick the door shut with my foot and walk carefully to the fire pit where Gramps is building a pyramid of wood, pieces he'd collected out in the desert on his last four-wheelin' trip. He balls up copies of last week's *Holtville Tribune* and stuffs them in between the wood at the base. He walks around the pit, bends down to light each ball. A half-smoked Kool dangles from his lips, ash occasionally dribbling down his thin blue shirt. He hadn't changed after work. The embroidered "Frank" on the circle patch is the only part that still looks fresh after all these years. Silkscreened across his back in Granny's perfect penmanship: "Let Frank fix it!"

• • •

Gramps is a mechanic. His shop is the only one in town. All the church ladies bring their Buicks in for service. When I was little, Granny made me sit in the chair across from her desk in the office and read a book while she typed invoices and did her figures on the adding machine. But I grew restless and wandered over to Gramps. He taught me how to check tire pressure when I was five. In first grade, he let me climb up on a stool, wipe the dipstick, and put it back in to check the oil. When I was seven, he gave me a screwdriver and a carburetor. It took me about six months before I could take it apart and put it back together to his liking. Granny made me scrub all the grease outta my nails before we went home to make dinner.

• • •

Gramps stares into the flames. Their flicker reflects in his pale blue eyes. I know he's thinking about my mother. His only daughter. He gets the same four lines between his eyebrows every time. He takes a long drag.

"She's not gonna show."

"She might."

"She never does."

He looks in at Granny standing over a bowl of hot boiled potato pieces, smashing in a steady rhythm. "She might."

I haven't seen my mother since I was five. She stopped by a week after my birthday on her way to or from San Diego, I can't remember. She gave me a pink flowered dress two sizes too small. Since then, she's been postcards and birthday messages relayed through Granny. Her face is a blurry memory. I only know what she looked like because of the family photos hanging above the piano. Her toddler self in front of the Christmas tree surrounded by my uncles ages five, seven, nine, and ten. School pictures in two pigtails, some with missing teeth, always the same lopsided grin that showed off her dimple. Her at about 14 in a hot pink swimsuit with two uncles on either side standing on the shore of the Salton Sea. I don't look anything like her.

Gramps finishes his cigarette and flicks the rest into the fire. He blows the kindling. Smoke moves into my face.

I blink hard, step back, and slosh a little sauce out the pot.

"Hey!" he scolds.

"Your fault." I walk over to the barbecue grill and set the pot down on its shelf. Sweat drips down the side of Gramps's already opened can of Schlitz. I take a sip.

He opens the grill and checks the coals. "If your Granny sees you . . ." He takes the can out of my hand.

• • •

There's a lot Granny doesn't see. By the time I get to Gramps's shop after school now, she's already finished the day's invoices, gone home to watch her soaps and make dinner. She doesn't know Peter walks me to the corner of Pine and kisses me on the cheek outside 7-11 then watches me walk down Fifth to the shop. Peter doesn't dare get any closer than that.

Granny thinks I go to the shop so I can use her giant wooden desk to do my homework. Which I do. She expects straight As now that I'm in high school. I always leave a trail of adding machine tape for her to see in the morning, even when I don't do math.

Really, I go to the shop to see Greg. He works for Gramps now that all my uncles have moved away. He has been pulling wrenches since he was 15 and I was barely in kinder. He broke up with his girlfriend right after I started wearing a bra last year. Coincidence? I think not.

Greg taught me how to change the timing belt on a Lincoln Town Car. My hands are small enough to mark the cogs without making a mess. His hands are twice as big.

But I can't have a crush on Greg anymore. My best friend Patricia said he's my dad's cousin. How does she know who my dad is when I don't? There are no photos of him with my mother. What I do know is that my dad was a soldier, went to Vietnam before I was born, and never returned. Not even in a body bag. Maybe he has a family there. Maybe I have a sister or a brother who speaks Vietnamese.

I asked after my dad once when I was about eight or nine, and Gramps threw the ice cube trays across the kitchen. He muttered curses and went outside for a smoke. Granny said some things are best left alone.

• • •

I collapse into one of Gramps's lawn chairs. The webbing scratches the backs of my thighs, the metal bar under my knee is cold. When he sets down his beer, I pick it up for another sip. It's warm. Gross.

Gramps turns the ribs and brushes both sides with beer and butter sauce. We only have these ribs and homemade biscuits on special occasions. Ribs and biscuits are my favorite. Granny has finished mashing the potatoes and starts making butter gravy, the kind everyone asks for at church potlucks.

"Don't know why Gran goes through all this trouble. Every. Damn. Time."

"Watch your mouth." He closes the grill and lights another Kool. Gets two beers out the back fridge.

I keep mine on the ground where Granny can't see.

Gramps shuffles and deals me five cards on the wobbly metal TV tray between us.

I shift my chair so he can't see my hand. Gramps cheats. I know from studying the red-backed cards in his hands that he has at least one Ace. That's not cheating. It's paying attention. Over the years, he has worried the corners of the Aces, never sure if he should go for the low straight or hold out for the high flush. I keep my three sixes. "I'll take two."

He grunts at me, sets his cards face down, and snaps two off the top of the deck. He gets up to turn the ribs over and brush them with beer and butter sauce again. Sometimes he uses this spicy mustard sauce that I don't like. Sometimes, he says, that's too damn bad.

I don't look at my cards right away. Inside the phone rings and Granny answers in her cheery voice, the one she uses when she has to call folks who owe Gramps money for a new transmission.

Gramps keeps only his Ace, takes four new cards, scowls at his new hand.

I watch Granny's face through the kitchen window. Only one person can change her smile like that. She slams the receiver back into the cradle.

"At least she called this time." I take a long pull from my can.

Gramps finishes his cigarette, drops the butt at his feet, then fans out his cards. "Pair of Jacks, Ace high."

Granny slams the cabinet door when she puts one plate away

and wipes her eyes with the back of her hand. She keeps talking like she'd never hung up the phone. Silverware crashes as she opens and closes the drawer.

"Should you go check on her?"

Gramps grunts again. Beer in one hand, tongs in the other, he gets up to open the grill cover. "Ribs are ready." He puts them on the empty cookie sheet, covers them with tin foil.

I fan my cards out on top of his. "Full house."

Granny lets the oven door close on its own. The bang startles her out of her rant.

We both stare at the back door.

I drink the last of my beer. "Think she's gonna come out here?"

"Go help her bring the food."

"Scaredy-cat."

"Not scared. Smart. I've been dealing with all that since before you were born. Now it's your turn."

I get the small, almost empty pot of beer and butter sauce off the grill shelf. It's cooling and has started to solidify a little at the edge. I lift the pot to my lips as I walk slowly toward the back door.

Granny ignores me, pokes the tops of her still-hot biscuits even though she knows they're baked to perfection. They always are. Without an oven mitt, she tosses each one into a towel-covered basket and folds the corners over the tops of them so they'll stay warm.

I set the pot in the sink, put the hot pad back in the drawer where it belongs, and wipe my greasy lips with a paper towel. I also use it to cover my beer burp.

Granny's still fussing with the towel, mumbles "ungrateful" and "irresponsible" and curse words I've never heard her say out loud.

I glance back through the kitchen window and shrug at Gramps.

He lights another cigarette and turns to brush the grill clean.

I hug Granny. Her whole body's tense. It's as if, after all these years, she expects my mother to be someone she's not.

HOUSES ACTING LIKE CARS

by
SARP SOZDINLER
Published in *The Masters Review*

There are two years between Pistol and Elwood, and Blue clicks into that gap. Yet she talks and walks faster than any of the boys in her hood—her friends can testify to that. Pistol looks as confused and genderless as that oyster he's carving the life out of with his father's old switchblade: a girl behind his shell; a boy in his glistening gold skin, with the curls of his copper hair combed back to the scalp and his baby-blue shirt untucked and two sizes too baggy from the waistband—his vision of perfection in another frame. Elwood, on the other hand, is an old soul stuck in a young man's body who has long lost the need for words and now talks only about his dreams full of tumors and horses as dark as his skin. He leads the trio forward with nothing but a grumble in his belly and a squish under his loafers en route to Drew Park, where Blue's mother used to pick her pastries and lovers from before she died of a combination of both.

Blue, as always, seeks Jesus, but in today's case, one Jésus Parejo, her father, the first of many, as printed on the flip side of the letter in her bag. Just the month before, a military-cut man who looked too white to be a relative and too old to be her friend showed up at her late mother's service and handed her the envelope with the heart-shaped logo of Social Services stamped on it. The skin on the back of her neck went cold as soon as she spotted the name on the first fold. She checked the print a few times, but the truth of the ink was absolute. The letter had a more personal vibe to it than some others she had to deliver during the day, a pearl of fate or a cut-rate omen she just couldn't afford to avoid. At sixteen, she still knew as little about her father as her job, from which she took the morning off to work up the courage and finally meet the man.

"Ariel would've loved that," said Mr. Pickering, her mother's childhood friend who'd offered Blue the spot at the post office on Pinecrest, filling his voice with a teary-eyed tinge. "See you all gussied up and responsible for a change."

Against Blue's expectations, her responsibilities are now stretching out in front of her eyes in the form of godlike buildings and sickly avocado trees. Spring is already halfway above the Tampa skyline, and wherever the trio takes, it is either a left turn immediately following a right or vice versa as if the city were mirroring Blue's confused mind. She can't understand how it's possible, but some roads keep returning to themselves as though her mother, with the help of some postmortem magic, concealed the traces that would lead to the man. Past a block or two, a series of condos and cubicles falls apart into an upper-class district only to regain its composure a few blocks later. Sidewalks start to smell of gasoline and old people, despite the thick film of rosemary cologne beaming off of Pistol's sunburnt neck.

"We're here," Elwood says.

The trio stops at the ivy-clad gates of a trailer park that looks misplaced and dispersed against the descending airplanes in the background. A glance at the park, and Blue cannot decide whether she's looking at cars acting like houses or houses acting like cars. Unlike the rest of town, there are no celebratory decorations within their eyeshot—definitely no flags, or anything in the spirit of the Fourth of July, or even remotely American. Only forgetfulness, abandonment, and poverty seem to thrive in this part of Florida.

"What is this place?" Blue asks and means it, too.

Pistol stops carving the oyster, but in truth there is nothing left to be carved. "Looks like a poor man's retreat if you ask me," he says, shaking his head, though Blue can't tell whether he's doing it in disapproval or otherwise.

At this time of day, Drew Park smells like alligator turd, although there are no crocodiles around this part of Tampa. Neither traffic lights nor street signs. There are a lot of trailer cars that orbit a majestic oak tree with its tall, priestly branches blessing the tenants under. Like all the other houses in the world, those trailers, too, were probably built with the promise of making one feel safe and secure at home but have failed to do so with their thin walls and lack of electricity or water service; the bathroom is an outhouse relocated every time the hole beneath fills up. Vintage vehicles are disbanded around. Roosters and chickens waddle in coops made of tangled copper wires and scrap wood. Doghouses named after dead movie stars. All in contradiction with how Blue has pictured her real father's life would turn out to be like.

Worse, the address printed on the flip side of the envelope leads her to a cartoonishly narrow singlewide that seems to be in worse shape than some trailers they have passed along the way. But unlike the rest, this one has a cross attached to its rooftop instead of a weathercock, and a flagpole for a lamppost in its front yard. Its walls are the color of rust, once possibly a shinier red. The porch is a bit tipped over, threatening to collapse on the passersby any second. An old Chevette seems to be retired from use between a graffitied sidewall of the house and a rusted-out shower cabin, missing all its parts but front wheels.

"Is anyone home?" Pistol asks.

"There's only one way to know," Elwood says, then lunges forward to knock on the door.

It was on a day like this a couple of months back that Blue waited at the doorstep of another house, her own, and watched the medics haul her mother's body onto a stretcher. Just a few minutes earlier, she was having her final vis-a-vis with that woman, who wasn't necessarily lively but alive. Blue sat down at the side of her mother's sickbed and asked about her birth father one last time, under the pained gaze of Baldwin, the last of many of her stepdads. In the past, her mother had skillfully evaded the subject but drunkenly joked on occasion how Blue's father was this "American greaseball" from North Carolina with "an earnest East Coast accent barbed as deep as the South goes"; the next second he would be a "hillbilly" from Kansas, "with hardly any meat to his bones." Blue didn't know what any of it meant, or whether the truth hid somewhere in the tangle of her mother's lies, but she eventually understood she would never get an answer, at least not the one she sought. So she left it at that, never to be resumed.

But that morning in bed, her mother just looked Blue in the eye until those eyes teared for no reason. An unintelligible answer popped out of her toothless mouth and then dribbled down her chin in the shape of saliva. The following moan and kicking about substituted the woman's crippled speech and rescued her from the burden of having to say something. Even when facing death, Ariel Beau's vocabulary functioned once again as her phantom limb, a manipulative extension of her mind games that Blue never knew how to deal with. In the seconds that followed, the woman Blue had known and loved as her mother turned from a fully formed person into a plant having difficulty wringing its armlike branches in front of her eyes. Blue, unsure of how to react, burst out laughing, in the same way she would when the Social Services man appeared out of nowhere like a genie and granted her long-lasting wish. Only then her future opened up before her eyes in a crystal-clear picture: Of course, with the kind of luck she had in life, her mother needed to get out of the way first so she could finally face the truth.

Blue now cups her hands around her eyes to peek through the screened windows and face what's left of her family. Family functions are supposed to be hard, but not one family member seems to be around to function with. Instead, the peephole remains one bright sun, filling more and more with light. White block letters kerning tightly along the threshold are warning any unwanted guests on behalf of the man, the brat pack included: INTRUDERS WILL BE SHOT AND SURVIVORS WILL BE SHOT AGAIN. Out of professional habit, Blue plays with the lid of a tin can mounted by the front door to accommodate mail, but it seems to be empty inside, like most things in Tampa.

Blue breaks away from her friends and steps out of the porch. Dry leaves crunch underfoot as she skims the length of the house. Between two neighboring trailers is an opening that leads to another backyard, where the grass is patchy with clay lump and cow manure and unearthing the true skin of the trailer park. In the canopy of an oak tree half a backyard ahead, she sees an old black terrier tied from its mangy hind legs to a mud-splattered Thermo King truck. The animal's body is scaly through furless pink patches, with her bulging ribs pronouncing the early traces of dehydration. Although some leftover chicken bones are loafing in the mud around his paws like browned bananas, the creature's eyes still plead for something proper to feed on.

"Can I help you, girl?"

Like a kid at the gates of a spook house, Blue cuts cold to the voice echoing from behind her. If she slips any sound at that moment, out of clumsiness or a heartbeat pacing a beat too fast, it's muffled by the uprush of blackbirds on the oak tree or the drumming of her blood in her ears. As she turns around, her body lets out a hardly discernible clicking sound in the stony silence of morning air, the impression of bones wrenching restlessly in a tense body. When she finally looks up, the voice presents itself as a barefoot, impish old man poking his head out of the back of the truck. He is puffing on his Pall Malls in his black clerical tunic with burn holes to match the constellation of moles on his face.

"I'm looking for one Mr. Parejo, sir," is all Blue can put together through a dry mouth.

Although nothing moves, something in the air flips off as soon as her words found a voice—an aspect of reality, the shade of sunlight, the gravity—filling everyone's mind with a portion of unease, including the dog.

"What about?" The old man's voice is like rocks breaking off the cliffs.

Blue tries to spot a resemblance in his accent, but all she gets is beer breath trickling from behind his graying fluff of mustache.

"I'm afraid that should stay between Mr. Parejo and I, sir." She takes one step forward and flips the letter in his direction; he bucks as if she's just drawn a pocketknife. The dog shows pulse for the first time and barks. The man's bald, bearded silhouette assumes an ungodly vibe against the sidelight beaming from behind the roof cross. He steps out of the truck to take a better look at the letter in her hands, and then frames Blue with a hesitant gaze. An air of suspicion wreathes his face even more than the cloud of smoke he exhales.

"Follow me," he says, flicking his cigarette toward the dog.

• • •

There is a time and place that stand out from where Blue's favorite memories as a kid are stored, and in all of them, in a dreamlike fashion, she's riding in her father's thirty-year-old Ford Bronco along the blacktopped guts of Florida. It may very well be a false memory, but she can vaguely remember the man reaching out to the backseat to fasten her seatbelt, and the more she pushes, the more the colors on his face crystallize into geometric shapes and then zoom back into a vagueness of features. Many a night, halfway between sleep and wakefulness, she tossed and turned in bed to conjure that man into her dreams. One day he would be a lanky, glassy-eyed businessman with a three-piece suit, and the next a sad middle-aged soldier. His face was a blank canvas that flickered from one shape to another all night long depending on each new description her mother had given earlier in the day, until one day it stopped altogether.

But she's never pictured him like this: a man of indeed no distinctive features, resuming his life spouseless, friendless, lifeless in a house the size of a prison cell, those four walls that seemed to have succumbed all sides of a person and made it an indispensable part of the concrete. Just like its owner, the singlewide looks far from its days of glory with its nameless species of off-colored plants, browned mirrors, and paint-flaked walls. Apart from some world maps and crosses hung here and there, there is nothing within sight that documents any sign of familial life—no dusty frames of an American family on the walls, no sticky notes on the fridge, and definitely no daughterly figure around. Instead, the minimum aspect of human existence is only on display through numerous yellow spots in the kitchen sink or those greasy fingertip marks on the windows as if breath has never touched this place or has abandoned it not so recently.

"I'll always have a bit of scatter at home," the man says after catching Blue's inquisitive gaze. "I'm not apologizing for it anymore."

Blue moves the junk aside on the burn-holed sofa to burrow herself a spot to sit; he takes the upturned laundry basket opposite her. She looks for traces of recognition on his face, but up close his face looks more like a piece of meat left out in the open for far too long. His orbital area looks particularly like one big breast, with a skin tag for a nipple.

"Would you like me to play something for you?" He stares up at her with level eyes. "I'm afraid I don't have much else to offer."

Blue nods, not knowing what else to do; she realizes she hasn't been breathing properly. The man gets up and walks over toward what seems to be a spontaneously formed hallway lined on both sides by crates. Soon he reappears with a cardboard box full of old vinyl records and cassettes and leaves it on the open kitchen counter with a thud. He removes a small tape player from a bundle of odd items and blows the dust off the machine. He fiddles with the switchboard that lost all its ink and then finds the right button after a few tries. The player haws out a mercurial zing, filling the ambient silence of the room with the sound of taped silence before the tobacco-tinged voice of Springsteen takes over.

"God, the voice." The man shakes his head in mock disbelief. "Slips right through your best defense every time."

Blue's mind is too preoccupied to compute his words; she's thinking about her mother and how she started to confuse Springsteen with Springfield nearing the end, how this was one of the first signs of everything that went wrong with her according to Baldwin. Yet Blue keeps this to herself, watching the man pull out of the box a fully green plastic GI Joe whose missing leg seems to have been replaced by strips of Band-Aid and a sticklike prosthetic gadget.

"Tell me, girl." He grabs a towel from the countertop. "What's your deal, really?" He swipes the layers of dust gathered on the toy's only good leg before leaving both the toy and the towel on the plinth of the player. "What brings you to this dump?"

Blue abruptly jolts up from the sofa and starts to roam about the room. The first-ever conversation they're supposed to be having as father and daughter hasn't been going anywhere near how she pictured it. All the words she has carried in her mind all day—all those years—even the gaps and commas in between, have now been resonating differently in the ambience of this strange house and against the face of this strange man. She feels overwhelmed with this need to touch everything she passes along the way to remind herself that this is her moment and it's real. From one of the windowsills she picks up this black-and-white picture of a little girl squeezed in a tiny wooden frame. The girl is a mousy brunette with a face similar to Blue's mother's, only much younger; she's staring away from the camera between three older kids, each being uncooperative in different ways. On the lower right corner, the photographer seems to have left his mark as the shadow of a peanut-shaped head while probably manning the camera.

"Let's say a friend had a dream," Blue speaks for the first time, then sets the frame back on the sill. "And in this dream, she had to watch her house burn up in big, big flames."

The man barely nods, his eyes on her.

"And, say, she'd like to learn what it was all about."

For a while, nothing moves in the room other than their heaving chests and sunlight. He stares at her, and she stares back.

"I think I can help you out with that," he says.

He pushes the stop button on the player and places it back in the box. He pats his hands against each other to mark the end of a job done and hauls the box right next to the bookcase. He reaches over and pulls an old tome from the top shelf full of leatherbound classics and textbooks. He blows the dust off the bony surface of the tome and flops his body back on the laundry basket. The spine reads, in golden serif letters, THE BIBLE.

"You see, girl," he starts hesitantly, "there are all sorts of fire in these pages if that's what you're looking for." He theatrically flips a page or two. "Bonfire, campfire, hellfire. You name it."

Blue nods in a magnetic trance.

"Why don't you tell me a bit more about this friend's dream?" he asks.

Blue switches her gaze between the man and the book to make sense of the scene but fails. "What do you want to know?" she asks to carry on with their little game.

He lodges his ring-clad fist under his chin. "Was the protagonist of this dream a firefighter by any chance?"

Blue shakes her head.

The man nods as if it explains a lot. He leafs through the pages one by one, and then in bulks. He pauses halfway through and tracks one of his bejeweled fingers down the page to pretend he's looking for something particular. "Care to tell me what kind of a fire was that?"

"Told you it was a house fire," she says.

The man glances up over the book. "See, girl, you're not exactly being very helpful here." He hooks a finger down the top of the page like a bookmark. "And God knows I'm trying my very best."

Blue's eyes go down like a lead balloon; she has long past her half-hour mark in this house, but it already feels like an eternity.

"So tell me"—the man clears his throat while crossing one leg over the other—"did this fire start on the roof? Was it the upper floors? The attic?"

"A full house, I'd say," Blue says in all her seriousness.

"Do you know if it was her own house or a random one?"

"Can't say for sure," she says. "Felt very much like hers, though."

The man is lost in thoughts for a moment. "See," he says, "in this case, I think there are only two sides to this story." He settles his face into the look of a doctor who's about to break some ill news. "None better or worse than the other, I'm afraid."

A hot flush creeps over Blue's face, reddens her cheeks.

"If it was a random house," he says, "then I'd certainly say it means that your *friend* is at last starting to find her place in the world."

Blue nods, gnawing on the insides of her cheeks.

"I'm talking about her connection with the rest of human-kind, you see," he goes on in the absence of a conversation. "Not necessarily in the sense of the whole world but still. It can be an existential barrier she may still need to break through. Or not. Who knows? You see where I'm getting at with this?"

Blue can't stop nodding, though she has no clue to what.

"She witnesses all these things unraveling around her and probably feels the pain of the longing for a family." Sigh. "You see, I don't even think this pain has to be channeled to her own family. That's not the point. The point is"—he looks up—"that she's finally beginning to slip into her own skin after so many years in the dark because she remembers she is a human being too and believes she deserves happiness like everyone else."

Blue wipes her cheeks with the back of her hand, which is damp and salty with running tears.

"But if it was *her* own house burning"—the man shuts the book in a puff of dust—"well, then I'm sorry to say, girl, but things start to change." He carefully places the book on the dirty gray rug and pushes it in the direction of Blue. "Because then it would mean this girl feels that her life has started to come down around her. You know, that someone made some decisions for her in the past and now she thinks they might be coming back to bite her. It means she's going through a period of her life where she feels like a complete ruin and that nothing is salvageable anymore. And you know what? It's probably true. She probably needs to rebuild her life to forget about it all. Move elsewhere, anywhere, and start anew."

He sighs like an engine dying in an old machine before locking eyes with Blue.

"Starting with a new family."

The sound of each breath is magnified in the glassy silence of the room. The dog barks on the other side of the window. Blue gazes about the room to do something efficient with her eyes. At first she gets used to the idea of looking at the man, then turns to look at the man, and lastly collapses on the rug like a windblown scarf. Her face jerks to left and right as if she's being slapped by a pair of invisible hands. Her feet kick about and stomp on the Bible along the way; the book swerves toward the far corner, where the crates are. The man does nothing, says nothing, and just watches the girl writhe on the ground for a few more minutes until she idles down to a state of stillness.

With a push on her knee, Blue stands up one leg at a time and wipes the saliva collected in the corners of her lips. She asks if she can use the bathroom but starts toward the hallway before waiting for an answer. After she closes the door behind her, she leans her back against the hardwood frame and feels the firmness of the handle on the small of her back. She swallows a gulp of air and kneels to throw up into the bowl. She flushes a few times to get rid of the smell, but those soupy pieces drifting in the low tide won't go anywhere. She removes her mother's pills from the breast pocket of her uniform and swallows them without water. She gets up to wash her hands in the sink and lets them shake for a while.

When she finally looks up in the mirror, she doesn't see anything there, at least not right away; it's just through the mist of her breath and the steam of hot water the image of a sixteen-year-old girl gradually comes into view with that same dumb smile she remembers very well from her mother.

• • •

"What took you so long?" Pistol says as Blue slams the door shut behind her.

Heads pop out of neighboring trailers to try and find fresh ways of looking at this uneventful way of living like ants scouring for crumbs of intelligence for wintertime. At the bottom of the porch stairs, Blue glances at everything in the park except at her friends; the sky has paled from yellowish blue to a bluish shade of yellow in her absence and brought a colorless face of civilization made of cardboard and scrap metal and lapsed parenthood into better view.

"You know, we were starting to get worried." Elwood sneaks a glance. "Worried for *him*."

Blue opens her bag to avert the attention and pretends she's busy checking the day's work. She hooks from the bottom of her bag the letter she was supposed to deliver to this man who was supposed to be her father. Between her fingers, the envelope feels almost airy, another sign that it's the words that lend most letters their weight and significance. The paper stock is similar to those of her unsent letters to her father, with its disjointedly venous grains representing the magnitude of her anger, coupled with a touch of stylish embossment for the proof of their financial well-being with her mother. If they had any voice at all, those feelings, it would have been concealed in the rustle and texture of the paper, that loud silence synonymous with the gravest of letters. But they can also be problematic at times, those letters. They can muffle what the words they carry want to deliver. So one has to pay closer attention—to hear out those senders. Curious, snail senders. Hopeful senders. Orphaned senders.

"You all right, girl?" Pistol rests a hand on Blue's shoulder.

"Please don't call me that." Blue says, taking a step back.

The sky splits open and comes to her rescue with a light fall of rain. Half a yard ahead, a rare beam of sunlight peeks through the clouds and sketches lines on the dog's miserable face. With each raindrop, the potholes around the dog's paws look more and more like small graves dug out for its impending death. Blue snatches the switchblade off of Pistol's hands and walks toward the oak tree to cut the rope that holds the old creature captive. Even after its new-found freedom, the dog doesn't move. It stares at her, and she stares back. It seems to have expected to die soon and couldn't care less now whether it is free or not, or even alive. Blue removes the letter from her bag, crumples it into a ball in her hands, stoops to dip it in one of the pooled holes in the ground, and feeds it to the dog. The dog gives in and hunches its neck to do as indicated.

"What's going on?" Pistol asks Elwood, who looks similarly confused.

Blue lifts the dog and places it behind the zipper of her uniform to protect it from the rain. She caresses the back of the animal's head as she flings her bag over her shoulder and walks back toward her friends.

"Men," she replies, pouting.

ITHACA IS NEVER FAR

by
SEJAL SHAH
Published in *LitHub*

The first time I kissed an Indian, it didn't feel like incest, and I was surprised. Maybe it was because we had blurred ourselves with cheap white wine in anticipation of the event—but I can't speak for him. Sure, I'm the product of two Indians—but one and two generations removed from the unpromised land, from dar-bath-shak-rotli in the kitchen every night. All the desis I knew were cousins or felt like it. Or they were like me and had a thing for blondes. I couldn't blame them, really—it's hard when you grow up here.

Well, sometimes I blamed them, my desi brothers; the very

best-looking ones were always sure to have a tennis player on their arms or behind their parents' backs. I scan the announcements to see if they are marrying these tennis players (and yes, some of them are). And what about me? The boys I go out with are scarecrows: working class Methodists or Episcopalians or rebellious trust fund WASPs. You've seen them around—they have an earnestness around the eyes, the nose like a kid drew it, a dog they love more than girls, the hope of teaching English in China someday.

Maybe I gave the Indian too much credit, because he didn't try to tell me stories about women in Rajasthan, thinly quoting the last article in *The New Yorker* or the *Times* that had to do with the plight of women or the horror of arranged marriages (so fascinating!) or the sanctity of the hymen or the supposed dowry problem. Perhaps he was tired of having such stories quoted back to him from smart Jewish guys at work or well-read tennis players anywhere— (airports, bars, weddings, dates). Maybe I should be telling this story to him and not to you. I don't mind if you listen, though. You: you could learn a thing or two.

Obviously he didn't taste like saffron, like turmeric, like asafetida. He tasted—you tasted—like the inside of a wine bottle, the green neck of a wine bottle. Your lips were surprisingly soft. You clearly wanted to forget about an old girlfriend and came quickly, damply, into your corduroys. I was embarrassed for you. We were out on a terrace, and I wondered who could see us. If there was such a thing as privacy in India, I didn't find it. If there is such a thing as divination, I misread it. We drank glass after glass and stayed outside though the insects hummed incessantly around our hands, our eyes, the rims of our smudged glasses. A near-empty carafe stared back at us. I thought: maybe this is the one.

Maybe I should try telling a more palatable story: about kissing a boy who had skin as brown as my brown skin, who worked in computers, who drank single malt with the guys from work, who listened to hip-hop, who wore a blue shirt the color of Friday casual, the color of desire. Maybe the problem is that *I* read the *Times* article. I thought we might fall in love, marry, have a story to tell our children. Listen kids: we met on the night train from Bangalore to Madras. Or: we met in Madras (now Chennai), but we first noticed each other on the night train. I pretended to sleep, to ignore the dosa-wallah, the coffee-wallah, the others on the wedding trip. I thought the coffee-wallah would return and he never did. How I wanted you to come to my row of seats and visit! And you did, after a time. Or maybe I should tell our children the truth: I had to come find you. You were talking to the girl with yellow hair, and I thought: this is it. You have found your perfect opposite. What could you possibly want with me?

What seduced me? Was it traveling with only one other desi on a trip of Americans and a handful of Europeans? It seemed that you were the only other Indian the way everyone nudged us together, left dinner early, pointed out your virtues, etc.—and of course you weren't the only Indian—we were in the ancestral home-land after all. More of us than I'd ever seen. Our parents called this place home perhaps, or had once called it home; we had this small fact in common. And we shared this fact with six million people or one out of six people or something rather unremarkable—maybe only remarkable in its easy probability that two of six million might find themselves staring past a carafe into each other.

Was it that we were going to a wedding? Or that you lived in that mythical city, New York, and that I was the age to be look-ing for myths—or that you had that familiar deviated-septum desi nose—or that you were South Indian (Brahmin, Tamilian), but didn't seem to hold it against me that I wasn't? Is it too scripted to suppose that brown chases brown? That brown is divinely meant to come together with brown? Where is the divination? Was it too much to hope that a night train from Bangalore to Madras might yield a good story for our children?

I suppose our children are still out there, but have gone on to be born to other people. When I told you I lived in Ithaca, you told me you didn't go further than Duchess County. (I thought probably you wouldn't make it past White Plains. Why did I kid myself?) It seemed pretty clear. We traded three phone calls and talked once, on my coin. It was the last day of October and kids had long stopped ringing the doorbell. That was all.

Children: your mother's mother traveled from Dar Es Salaam to Surat to meet her betrothed—on a boat that made her sick. She sailed a steam boat from one continent to another. Surely you understand why I can't marry your father—for him, Ithaca is far. You wouldn't like a father who cannot travel—who will not travel. How will we show you where you are from? Ithaca, Manhattan, Bangalore, Surat. I wasn't quite honest before. All the desis haven't felt like cousins. I'll keep trying. I just want you to be able to get back to the unpromised land, when you need to, when this whiteness is too much with you.

Oldest son: How will I be able to force you to take Gujarati lessons if your father is American? Who will remind you to take your shoes off at the foot of the temple when I'm tired and your sister is in my arms? Perhaps it will be your father, (thin, holding your hand, I can see that much in my mind), who will drive you to your Gujarati lessons, who will be more fluent than myself, who will not mind trans-Atlantic flights nor applying for visitor visas. Perhaps he will keep track of the lunar calendar and will remind me of when the harvest festival and the New Year fall each year—there have been times I've not even forgotten, but just not known. There are times I haven't been a good Indian. I have tried to be a good Hindu, to be your good mother. Each night, I unravel.

Forgive me, *beta*: I'm trying to make a good decision. I look for your dark lashed eyes, for your crooked smile, in each face, in every bar, in each set-up, trying to find your father, trying to recognize your laughter. How will I know if what you want is to be lighter, to be stronger—is to have a connection to Ireland? How will I know if what you are is half Jewish? My hand falters on the loom. First son: send me a sign, rent these fictions. What I'm wearing is red. What I'm looking for has already been written, what I can't read splays itself across the sky, nightly.

HOW TO
SURVIVE A
BLACK HOLE

by
DAWN TASAKA STEFFLER
Published in *Pithead Chapel*

I've been racing the sun for eight hours from LA to Tahoe. And I manage to pull it off, cresting Echo Summit just as the glowing orange ball sinks behind the mountains. My reward, as the serpentine road descends, is the great, green basin unfolding in the last of the dusky light: a place where my mother has said she wants to die, a place suffused with my older brother's ghost, where the lake is a silver mirror surrounded by thousands of pine trees.

It's too late to visit Mom, so I go to the house—a steep, pitched roof over beige siding with moss-green shutters and striped window awnings. I turn on the lights, and the wood-paneled walls of my childhood materialize, as does Mom's collection of bear tchotchkes, grizzlies and teddies, wooden, woven, ceramic, and stuffed. I had once asked Dad, "Doesn't this drive you crazy?" and he just shrugged his shoulders, "I can't tell her no."

Now he's been gone for a year, and except for the two times I flew into Reno, Mom's alone, too, with no logged visitors except for me—an endless stretch of days. Around a month ago, I decided. December isn't optimal, but I have four weeks off for Winter break. And the walls of my little apartment were already closing in on me. So I'm here to clear out the house and move her to a memory care facility closer to me.

A hole in the wall by the fridge draws my gaze. Twenty-two years ago, we sat on the hard pews of Community Presbyterian while the Pastor tiptoed around the fact that Tim put a gun in his mouth. And while we were in church, a bear entered through an unlocked slider, attracted by the smell of food laid out for Tim's reception, and demolished Mom's kitchen. It pressed the fridge door against the wall so hard that the handle embedded itself in the drywall. I run my finger around the time-smoothed perimeter, another one of Mom's precious souvenirs.

I spend the next two weeks sorting my childhood home into piles of keep, donate, or dump, and it occurs to me that this is an excellent example of a recursive algorithm for my undergrads: breaking down a problem into smaller and smaller subproblems until you reach a small enough problem that can be solved trivially. Still, there are moments I can't explain. When I box up Dad's tools in the garage, they feel oddly warm. Packing Mom's wineglasses conjures up all the nights she was drunk and tossing Tim's bedroom for a note he never left.

And Tim's bedroom. His cold doorknob reminds me of how I have found it easier to respond over the years, "No, I don't have siblings." Even though the walls have been blank and the furniture gone for years, I remember his posters of Hubble Telescope images, Mars, Saturn, and Jupiter. But also whirlpool galaxies and nebulas that looked like someone kicked over bottles of different colors of paint. The only thing left is a map of the night sky tacked to the ceiling over where his bed used to be. I recall lying on the back deck, Tim's finger tracing the constellations, telling me that the Little Dipper is also called Ursa Minor, The Little Bear. I lie on the floor and look up at the star map, searching for familiar patterns.

Finally, the house is empty, and it's time to drive home. I stop by Mom's favorite bakery before visiting her one last time. She's in the TV room, which feels like a geriatric drive-in movie with wheelchairs instead of cars. She protests when I wheel her away from the cooking show. Back in her room, she doesn't recognize me, and I can see the distrust simmering. Until I pull out the pink bakery box. Her eyes light up, and her twiggy fingers animate when she sees her favorite glazed, marzipan-filled bear claw. While she chews, I ask, "How would you like to go on an adventure? Move down to

LA, closer to me?" Like a small child, she bobbles her head up and down. I have no idea if she's responding to me or the pastry, but for the first time, I sense her cracking open. And I want to believe that decades of sadness and obsession can still fall away. Collect in her lap alongside all the almond slivers and shards of glaze.

On the way to the real estate agent's office, I realize I had left Tim's rolled-up star map in the front hall. The smell of something musty and wild bombards me the second I enter the house. Also, it's breezy and freezing. I tiptoe into the kitchen, and it feels like I'm sixteen again, waterlogged in grief, my mother screaming and my father holding her by the waist, trying to pull her away. The fridge is open, the cabinets are open, the sliding door is open. I grab the map, run back to my car, and sit there, heart racing, thinking about Tim and black holes and how the weatherman said this coming weekend, they were expecting the season's first snow.

THE HOUSE
ALWAYS WINS

by
SARA J. STREETER
한혜숙
Published in *Cutleaf*

As she pulls up to the house for the first time, Tess spots the white goat. It stands in the fenced-in side yard, chewing on tufts of weeds and watching as she steps out of the car. Grinding its mouth in a circular motion, the goat quickly loses interest in her. She debates whether to pet it but veers toward the house.

The front door is bloated and warped from years of heat and cold, the forest green paint in shreds. The knob doesn't turn, but with force, the door opens with a groan and a thump. It's dark inside except for a teetering floor lamp in the corner. The main room oozes the dank, stale smell of beer. Flattened boxes from cases of Busch Light cover dingy floorboards. A brick fireplace's gaping mouth devours more empty beer boxes, along with cigarette butts and a few empty bottles. A well-oiled Remington shotgun hangs above the mantle.

Garrett emerges from the other room and wraps Tess in his arms. "Hey, you."

She stands on her toes to kiss him, running her hands along his broad shoulders. They've been together for a year, but she still gets butterflies when he touches her. She likes Garrett because he's goofy, cute, and awkward—her favorite white-boy flavor. The same dumb puns, breakfast orders, and quiet moments together. It's comfortable.

Opening her eyes, Tess notices a yellowing Confederate flag tacked on the wall above a sectional with collapsed, stained cushions.

"What's up with that?" She points at the flag.

"It's Bobby's." He nuzzles her black hair. "Left over from when his parents lived here. He just never took it down." He tries to steer her away from the flag.

"And you're OK with it?" she prods him.

"Oh, come on, babe. It's just a flag. You know I don't believe in that stuff."

She bites her tongue. She doesn't want to start the weekend with an argument. As the son of conservatives, discussions about racism are simply not in Garrett's wheelhouse. She worried his parents wouldn't be able to wrap their heads around their son dating someone who wasn't white, but to her surprise, her race and their status as an interracial couple have, supposedly, been non-issues for his parents. It makes her feel like she is a non-issue too. She wonders if maybe they are just waiting out his Asian-girlfriend phase.

Garrett's bedroom is small but tidy. On the dresser, there are photos of the two of them from their anniversary at her favorite restaurant and his brother's wedding last year, both in Richmond, reminding her of how much fun they used to have when he lived there. Now Garrett's in Toano, worlds away from any nightlife. It's a dying small town rumored to be built on an Indian burial ground. Nothing feels alive there.

Garrett opens his top dresser drawer and points inside. She peers in and sees a clean toothbrush lying neatly on a paper towel next to a stack of folded boxers.

"You should keep your toothbrush in here too. Bobby never cleans the bathroom."

"I miss your old place," she says. "I mean, it was kind of gross too, but not like this."

"Bobby gave me a good deal on the room, and it's an easy commute to work. It'll just be until I figure out my next move."

Tess wonders what he thinks his next move will be. She wasn't thrilled when Garrett took the position updating computer software at the corrections facility. His first week there, a guy tried to stab him with a shiv made from two plastic sporks. "What can I say, some dudes want to spork me," Garrett chuckles whenever he tells the story. His new job, the crappy house, hurtled him backwards, away from the life together she imagined for the two of them in Northern Virginia. She would hang his artwork on the walls in their new apartment together, they would get a dog, and have happy hours with the nice couple next door. It would be perfect. She just has to get him out of Toano.

• • •

That night, she hears Bobby throw open the front door. His footsteps are full of booze, although he doesn't stumble. He slams his bedroom door shut. The house shudders, then sleeps.

• • •

The next morning, the living room is dim except for spastic light coming from a muted TV. Bobby sits at a folding table, cleaning the Remington next to an open Bud Light. It's a rare weekend off from his job at the 24-hour pancake restaurant. He greets the couple with jolly blue eyes and a wide smile.

"You must be Tess!" He sets the barrel down. He stands to give her a hug, and his embrace smells like gun oil, cigarettes, and a whiff of body odor. In an instant, Bobby's hands sneak below her shoulders, and she jerks out of reach. He gives her a boyish grin, the one she assumes he uses to get away with bad behavior. Not sure what to say, she shakes her head and rolls her eyes. Although he creeps her out, she remembers Bobby is Garrett's childhood friend and forces herself to gather her composure.

"I met your goat yesterday. What's its name?"

"That's Gloria." Bobby sits down and picks up the shotgun again, wiping it with a rag.

"Gloria? Cute. How long have you had her?"

He cocks his head. "My parents got her for me when I was 15 I think. She's awesome. If you want, you can feed her an apple later." He speaks with a tenderness, almost love, for the animal, then the moment passes. Bobby takes a sip of beer as he redirects his attention to the gun. "A few of us are heading out on the river later. Going to do some boat drinking on my day off." Garrett smiles at the invitation and, without looking at Tess, throws his oldest friend a thumbs up.

• • •

Water licks her body and sprays her face as the three of them speed out on the river in Bobby's motorboat. Tess has already lost count of Bobby's drinks, but she tells herself he's the kind of guy who can hold his beer. They approach a secluded strip of beach with ten boats tied up in a row. Bobby slows the motor. Through strains of Lynyrd Skynyrd and 2Pac, Tess hears laughter and the satisfying crack of cans being opened. Cigarette smoke and weed waft through the air.

Sunburnt guys with too many blurry tattoos stand waist-high in the river holding beer cans. In between sips, they ogle the girls on boats—a mess of bikinis, sunglasses, and loose flesh.

After they tie up, Tess climbs down to stand in the water next to Garrett. He slides his arm around her, and next to his tall frame, she feels protected from the gaggle of drunk white people. From under her sunglasses, she reflexively scours the group of partygoers until she finally spots another Asian girl, simultaneously relieved and annoyed to see her. The girl flirts with a group of white guys on the beach, who are clearly enthralled. Slender with black hair that kisses the top of her ass, the girl's string bikini clings to her bronze body like she was born wearing it. She catches Tess staring and abruptly looks away. Nearby, Bobby sees the direction of Tess's gaze. He crushes his can in a tight fist.

"I'd bet that one likes it rough," he mutters. "Chinese chicks will let you do just about anything." He roars with laughter at a joke that doesn't feel like one, his pale, wet belly jiggling in the hot sun. Garrett coughs loudly and tilts his chin towards the boat.

"Hey Bobby, that bottle of American Honey still in the cooler?"

• • •

Tess wakes up that night from an uneasy, alcohol-infused sleep. She hears a female voice in the living room along with Bobby and a few other guys. The girl's voice is soft and husky. Though she can't see her, Tess imagines her to be a box blonde from the river, complete with a "tasteful" Confederate flag tattoo on her ankle, tacky navel piercing from high school, lips prematurely wrinkled from a trusty pack of Camel Lights.

To quench her curiosity, she gets up to go to the kitchen. Gingerly stepping out of the bedroom, she sees the Asian girl from the beach sitting on Bobby's lap, a blank look on her face. Under a sheer mesh tank top, she's still in her bikini, long hair in a messy bun on top of her head, her spotless eyeliner now smudged and drooping. The girl attempts to stand but crashes down on Bobby, who greedily pulls her back into his lap. Two shaggy white guys on the sectional hoot and cough puffs of smoke. Tess pauses mid step when she sees a row of orange pill bottles lined up on the coffee table. Garrett mentioned Bobby liked to party, but she figured it was just the usual alcohol and weed.

Hoping to avoid being noticed, she steps lightly into the kitchen and finds a water bottle in the fridge. She takes a sip and looks out the window to see Gloria asleep in her pen, so peaceful and innocent. How strange that Bobby loves the goat so much when he doesn't seem to care about much else—not himself, not his house, and not the unfortunate girl on his lap. Tess's mind wanders and she considers barging into the living room, pulling the girl off Bobby and shaking her soft, narrow shoulders. "Wake up!" Tess would scream and, with that, the spell over her would break. The front door would fling itself open, and the girl would be whisked out the door, away from the pills, away from Bobby's house.

Tess caps the water bottle and slinks back to the bedroom. On her way, she sees Bobby whisper in the girl's ear, his meaty fingers inching up under her tank top. The girl nods and reaches toward a pill bottle. Tess closes the door, relieved to be back in the bedroom, safe with Garrett. The situation she just witnessed makes her shudder, but she doesn't want to get in the middle. It's better not to be involved; confrontation has never been her strong suit. Back in bed, she reassures herself before falling asleep.

Tess dreams she hears a barely discernible knock on the bedroom door. From the lumbering footsteps, she knows it's Bobby. Frantic, she looks at the door and sees it's unlocked. She hears Bobby go into the bathroom and slam the door. She hears him vomit, a guttural, ghastly sound, and she leaps to lock the door. When she turns around, Bobby's standing beside her in the bedroom, blue eyes glowing in the dark, outstretched fingers inches from her skin. She wakes with a scream burning in her mouth.

• • •

Back in Arlington, Tess finds she's desperate to clean the musty smell of the house out of her clothes and hair. It fades after a few days, but at night alone in her apartment, she thinks she hears Bobby's slow, wasted footsteps. Even in the crisp white walls of her modern apartment almost 150 miles away from Toano, she can't shake the house from her mind. Two weeks pass and she begs Garrett to come visit her, insisting the trip to see him wore her down. The truth is she can't go back to that house; it's haunted by a man who's still alive.

A month later, when Garrett tells her Bobby got fired from the pancake restaurant for being drunk, she pictures Bobby strumming his guitar in the dark, the pile of empty beer cases steadily piling up, his beloved goat growing thin and desperate—the man and his house held together in their decay.

• • •

Monday 10:11 a.m.: Garrett calls while she's in her weekly team meeting.

"He's dead, Tess. Bobby's dead." His voice breaks. She clutches her phone and hurries out of the glass conference room.

"What? Oh my God. What happened?" It comes out a fervent whisper.

"Heroin."

Outside, she sits down on a bench and stares at the sky. Her suit jacket starts to strangle her.

"Shit."

They stay silent, listening to each other breathe. It's over. The house wins.

• • •

When Tess pulls up to Bobby's house for the last time, the street is full of trucks with mud slicked on the sides, hatchbacks with Phish and FloydFest bumper stickers, old sedans needing paint. These are Bobby's friends, the people who loved him, and she's come to join them for the country boy's last rites.

It's beginning to get dark and as Tess gets out of her car. She's greeted by the smell of a bonfire and the familiar twang of blue-grass. Garrett squeezes her, a sad smile on his face. Her hand in his, he guides her behind the house to the people circled around the fire. The rag tag group eyes the newcomer as he seats her in the blue camping chair next to his.

"Hi," she says with a little wave. "I'm Tess." The fire crackles in response. A dreaded blonde guy across from her nods as he continues playing the guitar. Everyone else, clutching red plastic cups and cigarettes, ignores her introduction. Tess sits back. She gets it. They don't know her, and she didn't like Bobby. There's no use in trying to make friends. She's there to support her boyfriend. Garrett comes back and sets a cup full of a dark liquid next to her.

"Moonshine and Coke. Dan got it from a guy in the mountains last time we went tubing." She takes a sip and grimaces. "Go easy, it's strong." It's worse than rubbing alcohol, but she knows to drink it if she wants to get any sleep.

The evening goes on with music, drinking, and reminiscing. Tess pulls the hood of her sweatshirt up and takes big gulps, nodding along to the stories and jokes, even taking a hit or two from the bowl being passed around. As she reaches the bottom of her second, maybe third cup, she tears herself away from the fire in search of the bathroom. The living room is emptier and cleaner than she could have ever imagined. It's almost unrecognizable. The flattened beer boxes are gone, and there is only an outline of where the Confederate flag hung on the wall for all those years. She wonders who cleaned, maybe some of Bobby's friends or his family. Tess shudders thinking about what they found—beer cans and bottle caps, stray pills, cigarette butts, mouse droppings. God knows what else.

The smell of stale beer lingering in the house begins to turn her stomach as she reaches the bathroom. She closes the door and presses her forehead against the grimy mirror. She knows if she pukes she'll feel better. Holding her hair away from her face as she hovers over the toilet, she recalls Garrett's warning about the bathroom and tries not to touch the seat. The sound of her retching echoes in the tiny room. She wonders how many times Bobby must have thrown up right there, in the same bathroom. She wants to be sad about his passing, but she can't. His death, the heroin, it all felt inevitable.

When it feels like everything is evacuated from her stomach, Tess rinses her mouth and splashes her face in the sink. She walks out of the bathroom on wobbly legs towards Garrett's room, where he's staying until the end of the month. They've looked at a couple of apartments near her place in Arlington, but they have yet to agree on any of them. He always finds something wrong, the timing, the deposit, the smell of the lobby. Tess worries he's not going to grow up, and Garrett thinks she's pushing him too hard, but mostly they argue about the high cost of living and shitty Beltway traffic. She realizes the end of their relationship is probably inevitable, too.

Something behind her makes a sound. She freezes. She hears it again, unfamiliar footsteps, closer this time. She turns slowly. Standing a few paces away is the goat, silhouetted by the dim light behind her. Gloria looks at the human curiously. Tess exhales with relief.

"Gloria, old girl. What are you doing here?"

She extends a hand, but the animal backs away. A wave of laughter rolls in from the open window reminding her of Gloria's former owner.

"Bobby's gone, sweetie. I'm sorry." The words come out before she can catch herself. Oddly enough, she finds she means them. The goat takes another slow step back and then another. Tess is surprised by the thick, muddled emotion she has for the animal. Was this what Bobby felt for her? Through Tess's wasted state, a thin line of resolution appears; Bobby is free, and now it's Gloria's turn.

She carefully leads the goat to the empty living room and opens the front door. Bugs buzz and flock toward the light. Gloria saunters to the threshold and hesitates, sniffing the cool, crisp air. Tess smooths the animal's coarse pale fur as together they take in the night.

"Go on," she says softly. "Get out of here."

FIELD METHODS

by
LISA WARTENBERG VÉLEZ
Published in
Michigan Quarterly Review

Thirty-eight bodies lie arranged across the three and a half acres of Jumping Gully grassland in various stages of decomposition. To encase the cadavers, Miriam attaches chicken wire to the four metal stakes, two to flank the feet and two above the head. Anytime Miriam hears the word blistering from now on, this image of amber-colored flesh will slice into her consciousness. She still likes soil against her skin but soon gives up meat.

Miriam's ongoing project since the beginning of the summer involves helping a doctoral student named Brittny track how clothing affects the ways in which vultures feed on a decomposing body in a field. Wildlife and a trillion putrefying microbes render the postmortem interval visible. Florida has a thousand-person back-log of unidentified victims. The project's reconstruction of a crime scene makes use of the natural world as an informative witness, a corroborator to justice.

Most cadavers that arrive fresh at the body farm are laid out su-pine, reminding Miriam of a yoga pose from the class at the country club where her mother works. Glossing up rich gringas is how Pilar puts it. Decay weathers holes into certain torsos while distending or bursting open others, maggots ravaging at the waxy insides. On some faces, a black line called tache noire marks the open eyes, the retina like a crossed-out O, like the Greek symbol theta, or the X-ed out eyes of a dead cartoon character. Miriam can understand why, as Dr. Weiss explains at the dry lab, theta is used as the symbol of death.

Miriam likes how clinically these bodies present; it helps her think of them as specimens or dummies rather than the marbled dwellings of former people. She imagines the shocked reactions she will get at parties when she describes what she does and preemp-tively enjoys the implications of her toughness, but in the darkness of her dorm room she can never not think about the small woman whose body lay angled in fetal position. Miriam—who prefers Miri now—spent her summer observing how the bodies fare against the elements and predators; now she is learning to excavate and clean skeletal remains, to inspect for signs of trauma.

• • •

A few weeks into the fall of her freshman year, Miri flips the channel to static and stares at the peppered screen at the foot of her bed. Her roommate, Ashleigh, is an affable communications major with a boyfriend, a swimmer named Jonah. Earlier that night Miri thought she overheard them making fun of her. From the giggled whispers she sussed out, her offenses are that she doesn't flush after she pees, that the birth mark on her cheek looks like mud, and that she never leaves. Ashleigh and Jonah are always leaving——to a party, to a meet, to a date.

Miri lies in the darkness of the still-strange bed, plastic mattress cover crinkling beneath her weight as she shifts to warm her shoulder with the too-thin blanket her mother bought. She hopes this won't be yet another night when Ashleigh and Jonah hook up in the bed just four feet away from hers.

Miri does this a lot, this lying here, listening to static when she's alone. She can hear him then, her dad, if she listens closely enough. She's been listening closely enough for eight years now, to the speckled sounds meld and scatter, then repeat themselves into meaning. At times it sounds like the telephone from her old house, its round sound, its drag at the second ring, or like the grade school bell. Other times, it mushes together like the hum of his car engine. Tonight, when her dad's voice finally shapes itself from the mound of static and she hears his Mi chiquita, her mind sputters. She forgets what she wanted to say to him. This has been happening lately. Maybe, Where did you go? or Tell me how to find you but she can't seem to organize her thoughts. She is too tired to journal. She is too tired in general. The forensics internship is designed for seniors, not freshmen, but her mom's longtime client's friend runs the program and got Miri in before the summer to fill a vacancy. And now here she is, busier than most of her classmates, more miserable probably, unsure if she's heading in the right direction, unable to tell her dad about it in her secret ways. The wrong parent died she thinks, in her less generous moments, in moments like this one.

When Miri drifts off, she dreams of him for the first time in weeks. Maybe it's a memory relived? Burgers frying in butter, her mother's bare feet on a kitchen rug the colors of America, his laughter grainy through the land line in their kitchen, her finger coiled into the cord of the phone. Sapo verde, chiquitica, he would say even on days it wasn't her birthday, their joke. Don't wait up, I'm sorry. Him not showing up was also buffered through joking, and by her calling him Casper—but the irony was too much these days.

Miri opens her eyes to the pile of Ashleigh's laundry silhouetted by streetlight pushing in past half-closed blinds. She wills herself to see her father's shape there instead, a heap of concern even in afterlife. "Visit me," she says out loud. She is worthy of ghosts.

It's the middle of the night but Miri needs a shower. Afterwards, she brushes her teeth, wipes the fog off the mirror––alcohol and newspaper like Abuela taught her––scrubs the toilet, disappears the pink ringing the sink drain, grinds a toothbrush against the grout, watches the brown turn yellow and then white, and at last her chest swells with her first full breath that day. She showers again.

Ashleigh's lipstick lies in a pile of earrings in the bathroom. Bloody Mary, says the sticker. Miri licks the toothpaste from the corners of her mouth, runs Ashleigh's crimson lipstick along her lips, and shapes them into a smile. She traces her birthmark with her fingertip. Café con leche, her father would say, or Geographic. She opens her mouth as wide as she can, watches the milky brown mark distend against the rattle of the mirror from the A/C. She wants to transform, but into what? A vulture, maybe. She worms into bed.

Ashleigh doesn't get home until that morning. She sits by their galley-style dorm kitchen below the buzzing fluorescent lights, eating a chicken drumstick with bare hands. Miri slumps sleepy over coffee, her lips stained red, and wants to ask about any parties going on that night but watches the steam rise from her cup instead.

Ashleigh pulls against the grayish muscle fibers with her incisors and uses her free hand to dredge the chicken in hot sauce. She plucks a cartilaginous end apart from the flesh, lays the thick yellow tissue on a napkin, sucks at the ends of her fingertips. She wipes her hands against her jeans. She wants to know about the body farm. "Tell me everything," she says, splaying her acrylic nails against the countertop. Miri digs into her cuticles with her teeth and notes Ashleigh's voracious mouth, her arched eyebrows, her too-white teeth.

"It's um––the bodies." Miri bites her bottom lip. "They're bodies. It's not *SVU*, I mean, that's what everybody thinks––it's, no, it's stranger than that. We don't get the stories, the whys. Just the bodies. We piece things together based on where they come from, like the hospital or the county morgue, what the body itself tells us. And it's like just––the way they rot there, what happens, it's––"

Ashleigh looks unaffected, a tinge of daring curls on her cheek. Miri would not be gentle.

"Sometimes a body is hurled out of a car, an OD, a hooker. Dumped like trash." Miri swallows, rolls up her sleeves, recalls the first time she threw up––the maggots, the flies like an iridescent sheet, the aroma of death that clung to her that week. She couldn't eat after seeing the man whose forehead looked just like her father's if life had let him age, but none of them were her dad, and she cried in her car on the way home, and vowed to be different, better than her mom, a good person—she just didn't know how she was supposed to do it without him.

"I can't tell you the worst of it or you'd never sleep again." She thinks of a chapter heading in her econ textbook, The Cost of Living. And this from a forensics handbook, Section 691, Provision 2 in the Health and Safety Code: the county may deliver unclaimed bodies as an anatomical gift in the absence of the decedent's identity, known relatives, or funding. So even death doesn't spare you from transaction. Even in death you can lose the tenderest part of yourself.

Ashleigh shifts in her chair, looks intrigued, says "Okay."

"Well, so. Four minutes after you die, the body begins to, to decompose. We smear camphor on our nostrils. But even then. The death smell. It doesn't really leave you. And sometimes you can see the fresh ones twitch. They bloat, explode, get picked apart. They melt into the earth. Like——we become different things. Even in death."

At this, Ashleigh whoas, lets her jaw hang loose, as if performing morbid intrigue rather than feeling the actual tug of curiosity. Miri imagines her on a game show glowing beneath neon lettering, her mouth agape with exaggerated surprise at having won the big prize. Then she imagines Ashleigh, her face frozen in wonder, cold on a receiving gurney. Next she's on one of those teen dramas, cast as a girl-next-door type who looks pretty even when she cries. Who smells like flowers after a run. Whose drama du jour involves two invitations to prom. Who would Miri be in this show? Probably Teen Nerd 2 bobbing in the background, tripping over her tray, plotting in which air vent to plant the stink bomb while lying on the tile. She burrows a finger into the back of her T-shirt and picks at a scab. She's covered in mosquito and horsefly bites these days.

"You should totally sneak me in sometime," Ashleigh says.

Miri smirks, almost nods. She doesn't know if Ashleigh is serious. Maybe she just wants stories for Jonah.

Jeans, the forensic team found, are protective to the flesh

against birds of prey, Miri explains. But jewelry entices them. These bodies, unlike the first group Miri handled, lay open to the elements, their decay videotaped. Then the footage was condensed and played on a Dell laptop for a huddled group of law enforcement from neighboring counties under a white pop-up gazebo amid tall grass and lifeless bodies. Even this cluster of hard-faced pros ooohed and aaahed and winced at the movement of the vultures: sometimes two, three, twelve composed the wake, a murmuration of decay, contracting and expanding like an organ of the earth to whittle the body down to the bone. Watching their faces last month, Miri decided a group of cops is called a gawp, but she shared that joke with no one.

We are fruit, she thinks, biting into her cuticles.

"How do you do it?" Ashleigh says.

Miri shrugs, thinks of her father. A person seven years missing is presumed dead. An un-embalmed body eight years postmortem is bone or is dust. Diagenetic. Unless he was sucked down into the bottom of Deep Lake after all. They'll probably never know how it went down——police only ever recovered his car off the shoulder. No hunting gun. No sightings. Phone missing, before GPS. Wallet intact, cinnamon leather bright against the gray seat; that spot along the seam, where their tabby had gnawed into the stitching, blaring white.

When she was twelve, a year after his disappearance, she lay flattened by a punch on the playground. Above, clouds spun. With him around, clouds would have shifted into lions or faraway horses.

But past the daze of the hit, Miri saw nothing––masses of gas and atmospheric patterns she would be tested on next week in science, a smattering of cumulus and nimbus. Bunching up a sweatshirt sleeve, she blotted the thick red trailing down and dotting the sandy loam. Her aggressor, Savannah, had marched off by then, flanked by an entourage of four metal-mouthed girls, leaving a redolence of Bath & Body Works sprays––Savannah, whose sixth grade mission was to eradicate her own elementary nickname, Dump Truck, by beating up anyone in their grade who let it slip out, as Miri had done, to the artsy eighth graders the week prior.

Miri stumbled to her feet. She fished out whatever of hers she could from the trash. But Janie's scrunchie––no sign of Janie's scrunchie. Her stolen relic from gym class, where Miri spent half of her time trying to bump into Janie, the only cool girl to smile at her after her mother's affair rendered her untouchable. She raked through the refuse and the tattered schoolwork in search of its mint green, its soft cotton, its dizzying scent––the indecipherable joy of Janie––but came up dirty and bare-handed. She tamped down the cheese and Wonder Bread bubbling from her belly from lunch several hours ago, eaten in the pointed solitude that is a packed middle school cafeteria.

• • •

Except for the building manager, Miri is alone at the lab. She's not supposed to wear her hooded sweatshirt beneath her lab coat, but it's Friday, and with most of the research team away at a conference, Miri finds pleasure in breaking this rule. She hovers over a worktable at the lab adjacent to the body farm and prepares a tooth sample for Dr. Weiss——powdering down a molar with a Dremel, scraping the snowy dust into a test tube. The chemical isotope analysis helps them learn about the subject's diet and environment. "Advanced stuff," Brittny had said, training her on the procedure last week, with an endearing enthusiasm that made her star-shaped earrings bounce against the back legs of her glasses. She has been giving Miri more to do since she learned her charge has declared a major in criminology. Miri wishes she'd had Brittny around growing up.

It's an intake day, the hospital morgue said this morning. A cancer death. Another grad student would be here at the intake, she had promised the assistant over the phone; she was just old enough to do it on her own legally, but it was against internal policy. Still, she inventories the steps, locates the manual in her mind, ensures the conveyor ramp is free of obstructions.

At noon Miri sheds her lab coat and walks to the orange metal picnic tables. She prefers to sit inside, but the smell of formaldehyde from an organ sample has made her lightheaded. Her skin bristles. She eats a hummus and avocado sandwich, holding her body tight against the early cold front. She takes out her private notebook, in which she documents the burgeoning case of her missing dad—— mostly fiction——and titles a new entry "The Reticulated Python Theory," forcing her inner voice to outshout the imagined criticism from her Field Methods professor. As she writes, she notices the dusting from the sample on the corrugated sleeve of her sweatshirt and feels the bottom of her stomach knot. A gray-and-white cat rubs itself against her legs. She pinches a sliver of cheese from her sandwich. As she lowers the offering, the stray scrapes the mound off her fingertips and darts off.

The body arrives. She has lost her appetite anyways and throws the rest of her sandwich away. After the grad student signs and sees the dieners off, Miri stares at the doughy flesh—–blood-pooled, discolored, and stiff but retaining the echoes of life. Uncanny valley. A person and not. A corpse and not. She thinks of how some things you become without trying, or despite trying. She spends most of the afternoon cataloguing and photographing before storing her, it, in the cooler. Dr. Weiss will be in tomorrow.

Miri hears the lab phone ring. She rinses her hands and wipes them against her sweatshirt. By now the grad student has left. When she holds the receiver against her ear there is only a dial tone. She looks at the caller ID but it is blank, like nothing. She stands there listening into the cold, thinks she hears static.

Hello, she wants to say. Are you still out there?

She is reminded of Pilar calling the sleepaway camp office on a long-distance card every afternoon and how whenever other campers asked, she would say it was her dad calling. That whole two weeks, Miriam never figured out how to tell her mom she had gotten her first period. As if by shedding the girlish version of herself she betrayed something. Left her dad farther in the distance. And as if, maybe, he wouldn't recognize her if he ever came back. In order to tack on camp to the end of Miriam's summer visit to her grand-parents in Colombia, Pilar had scraped together all she had, traded salon for boxed hair dye, daily contacts for glasses, glossed acrylics for unkempt hands during the several months leading up to the two-year mark of his disappearance. Miriam didn't see the sacrifice, only that her mom looked a little drab, which is what she had said the morning Pilar drove her to the airport, and she attributed the drabness to grief or age. Her mother's love was steadfast, but hard and quiet. Miriam wished her mother had just said the quiet parts out loud. How they'd both been resentful of his being gone, and that resentment became directed at each other.

Miri forces herself to hang up this phone. Walks into the lab cooler, its air icy against her temples. The body is there, mostly draped, the blush of life still apparent at the cheeks, the mouth, the hands, the parts laid bare.

At that sleepaway camp in Colombia, Miriam started a game that involved candy and trivia and punitive lipstick smears on the shoulders, face, stomach, thighs. Whoever got the most answers wrong, Miriam announced, would get a spanking. The blonde one, Isabel, from America like Miriam, got asked how many states there were. When the girl said fifty, Miriam shouted, Didn't you hear the US got more? We've had 52 states since 1983, stupid. Miriam raised the plastic clothes hanger in the air and brought it down against the bulk that was Isabel, who dove beneath the pillowy duvet. Miriam and her friend giggled at first as Isabel play-screamed, but then Miriam did it again, harder, grunting with the final blow. Folded up in fetal, it became apparent how childlike Isabel's proportions were. Isabel got quiet. Her breath hitched. Miriam set down the hanger and pretended to need something from the camp kitchen. We were just joking. Jesus, she said on her way out.

Miri stuck her head in the refrigerator and wished she could seal herself inside it. She had ruined it, she thought, this having friends, this popularity touristing. Sauntered to the bathroom and locked the door. Crouched on the floor, she caught herself hoping in earnest her father might call––caught herself forgetting all of it–– the cops, the search, the waiting––imagining him at home like he should be, listening to a record on their couch––and felt right then like she lost him all over again.

From the cooler, Miri watches her breath cloud and checks the clock. Nearly four p.m., still Friday. Lunch has worn off and her lids begin to feel heavy. Every few hours she is supposed to call security so they can watch her from the cameras as she walks the premises, documenting weather metrics, observable changes in the necrobiome, external signs of decay, and evidence of wildlife—but what about trespassers? Curious teenagers, homeless people, stoned college kids, supposed satanists. All of these could prove counter-productive to the study's efforts. They need decay to be the work of chemistry, the elements, and natural predators, not people.

How unlike life, Miri thinks.

The earth involves itself in death's work. At first death stains the dirt, deems it barren once the flesh and the bones dissolve into the soil, if not consumed by roving bugs, or birds, or other animals. Nourished, earth blooms. Brittny taught Miri to discern the evidence of long-absorbed bodies by the presence of taller, thicker foliage and a wider variety of bugs. About a third of the land allocated to their research sits seemingly empty, but it is hard at work. Before she can take off for the weekend, Miri visits the woman in fetal and wonders if she's there because of a desire to advance science or because she was broke. Miri notes the changes: newly receded nail beds, splintered fingertips, white fungus along the arm, deep amber hue across both tights.

Miri thinks she hears the faint bell of the phone ringing. She gets an uneasy feeling, like hearing strange noise in an empty house. She surveys her surroundings. Stiffens, like the fresh body now black at the feet. Walks up to its side and places a dried leaf over each eye. She sees no one––not a car except her own and the security guard's down the gravel road. Something grazes her leg, and she jumps, letting a stifled scream escape. The cat. She bends down to pet it. When the cat looks up, she notices its mouth is speckled with blood. It dashes off diagonally and hovers when it reaches a cadaver. Miri isn't supposed to stop them, so instead she looks away.

• • •

At her dorm late that afternoon, Ashleigh is already drunk, the boyfriend nowhere to be found.

"Jonah broke up with me" is what Miri untangles from the cries. She drops a box of tissues on the bedside table. Listens to Ashleigh wail about Jonah rushing a frat and Ashleigh not quite ready to go the sorority route, and from here she simply watches the mechanics of Ashleigh's mouth in motion, fat tears slaloming down into its corners.

"I need a distraction," Ashleigh says to Miri, with a pout and smeared lipstick, a bit pathetic now. Although Miri has never been broken up with, has never entered a relationship from which to be released, she feels a tug of sadness for her roommate that surprises her.

"Ice Cream? Taco Bell?"

Ashleigh's eyes glisten. "Let's go see the bodies!"

"It's almost dark," Miri says.

"Please?"

"I could get fired."

"We wouldn't even need to get out of the car," Ashleigh says. Miri hasn't noticed the sharpness of her roommate's collarbone before, how it cuts against the air, hasn't admitted to herself that she'd like to press her mouth against that hollow.

"Come on. Please?"

Ashleigh is crumpled on the bed, all knees and elbows and heels.

Miri bites her cuticle. Lets pleasure slip onto her face. Ashleigh is used to having her way, and so before Miri's shoulders sag and her mouth sighs out a "Fine," Ashleigh is already clapping her fingers together and fetching her designer purse.

• • •

They stop at the guard's window, an apology hunching along Miri's spine, her fingers curled over the steering wheel. "My backpack," Miri says, smirks like *isn't that just like me.* As if the guard would know. Not even Miri knows.

The guard scratches at a Sudoku and waves Miri in. She parks on the opposite side of the building and sits in her mother's old Passat. Ashleigh pops out from the leg space in the back seat.

"Let's just wait a little till it's full dark. The cameras," says Miri.

"I'm thirsty."

"I think we got maybe fifteen minutes."

"There's a party tonight if you wanna go. We could dress you up, if you wanna."

"Won't Jonah be there?" Miri's pulse raises. A college party, her first.

"Jonah who?" Ashleigh blows a raspberry. "Don't ever get a boyfriend."

And then: "Mir, do you believe in ghosts?"

Mir. Her spine tingles at the intimacy.

Miri doesn't answer but her heart begins to race. Feels the

grasp of this, this coming here, as a bad decision wrapping around her throat. She feels like a ghost of herself, floating above her own body. Not quite there, not quite not. She wants to launch herself out of this car, lie down in the field, let herself dissolve into the ground. Or she wants to walk into the ocean, commune with the infinite.

She looks back at her roommate. Ashleigh still pools into the footrest, her arm hooked around the bottom edge of the car seat and her head angled in repose. She looks angelic. Although her eyes are closed, she doesn't breathe like a sleeping person. Miri fumbles with the volume dial, lets it ride on the static from an AM station while she shuffles her MP3 player. She watches the sky glow.

"Hey, Ashleigh?"

"Mm-hm."

Miri thinks about her father in the field. She shapes her mouth into a word shape, a word like Lazaro, his name, not like she ever called him that, but she can't make the sound to carry it out of her mind. Tell me, she thinks, how I didn't die when you did. She doesn't talk about him, not ever. Not even with her mother. Especially not her mother: He liked guns better than people, she would say to Miriam, incapable of disposing his stash in their closet, and resentful of both the stash and her own incapability. Her mother, with her At least I stuck arounds, her steely argument killer, but of late, a blade that's lost its edge. Her mother who fixes the skin of the rich for a living, with endless patience for her clients' gossip and gifts, with her gin martinis every night, who cries on Miri when her dates don't show. But who makes her tea when she cramps, sneaks her samples of that good cream, her mother. For all her faults, she never has once disappeared. At least not like that. Not like him. Miri doesn't allow herself to think of her mother when she sees the woman in the bent-up shape wither, shapeshift. Doesn't allow herself to think of leaving the world the way you entered it. Penniless and afraid.

She feels jealous of Ashleigh. She'll never need that kind of heartbreak, not the boyfriend kind. The heartbreak of her father leaving will never heal and it's enough for her to carry. What Miri wants is a life gentle enough to accommodate the smaller aches.

After a while Miri says, "I think it's dark enough now." She thinks she hears the phone ring from out here but it's probably in her mind.

Ashleigh rouses, looks around through mascara-ringed eyes.

"You are gonna get me in so much trouble," Miri says. She could lose her internship for this. Her future. Maybe it would be worth it. What's a future without friends, anyhow? She was already tired of the smells, the maggots, and the way her fingertips—from soil or freezers or touching the dead—were perpetually cold.

She pauses the tapping of her fingers against the dashboard. Spies a vulture atop the fence outside smoothing its feathers. Ashleigh hiccups.

"Just to look," Miri says.

Ashleigh lays her tongue out of her mouth and gives Miri

a death metal fork with her hands. Against a look of warning, Ashleigh grins and pushes herself out of the car.

• • •

When they enter the lab, the woman in the fetal position is photographed in a binder, splayed open, on Miri's station. Ashley gawks and meanders to a cabinet of organ samples, as Miri rushes to shut the binder. She holds the image of the woman in fetal in her mind, the body curling into itself as the vultures circle, meld, disperse. She thinks about a photo from her textbook of a fire victim in pugilistic stance, like a boxer at the ready, trying to fight his way out. What if life only lays out these two choices?

Looking at the heavy grey-blue door with a small window cut into it, Ashleigh arches her eyebrows, crystalline eyes aghast. "Is this—is this where they put the dead bodies?"

"The new ones, anyway," says Miri, playing at insouciance.

Ashleigh presses her hands against her mouth like the Munch painting Miri studied last year. No, like the kid in *Home Alone*. Standing on tippy-toes, she mouths the words "Oh my God."

"They can't hear you," Miri tells her. "Well, we don't think, anyway."

Ashleigh loses her balance and catches herself on the metal counter.

"Do you—do you want to touch her?"

Ashleigh gets quiet. She nods her head.

Miri gives her latex gloves, unlocks the cooler door, and lets her inside the space, big enough for only a corpse and an attendant. Closing it, she watches Ashleigh through the window, seeing the body: its bald head, cavernous mouth, the wholeness of it, long like an arrow on the gurney. Miri fingers the key in her hand. A thrill swirls in her gut. She considers locking Ashleigh in. Imagines the look of disbelief on her face before panic sets in, the nervous laughter before the pounding fists, Ashleigh flying out of the cooler and shoving Miri against a wall, holding her by the shirtsleeves but holding her all the same, the crackle of static between two bodies, Ashleigh's hand soft on the back of her head, lingering there like her Dad guiding her at the hunting rifle, how he'd force her head to look at the gore while she tried to pull back, to look away. Or she could keep Ashleigh locked inside the little room forever like an angel in a snow globe. To keep life from shattering her.

Miri catches her own reflection, her birthmark superimposed on the glass like a stain. Like a country of its own.

When Ashleigh looks up and through square window, her face is transformed into a topographical map by the wire grid embedded in the glass.

"Wow," says the wide crater of Ashleigh's mouth.

"Yeah."

Ashleigh softens. Places a hand on her chest. Miri watches it rise and fall, Ashleigh's breath visible in the cold.

Miri feels the kick of her heart and imagines her blood pumping through the whole of her, the rush of molecules in oxygen conversion. Curls her hand around the door handle and opens. Cold yawns out against the edges of her skin. If Ashleigh were soil, Miri would burrow herself inside. Lie fetal until nature feasts on her remains. Transforms her into something better, something better than this. She thinks of the memories foregone, the ones that aren't memories at all, not hers, not anyone's maybe, or maybe not anymore, that hazy infant joy—the first tenderness, her breath against her mother's neck, her father's shoulder. She wants her body to speak, to tell her those stories, to hear her feet were once caressed by warm water.

PRINCETON

---

by
ROBERT YUNE
Published in
Avery and *Impossible Children*

I wasn't aware of resonant frequencies, how the right vibrating pitch can shake buildings apart. I was ten and all I knew was that our father was surrendering us. We had the sense of being carried to the end of the world, to this new, forested edge of New Jersey. My brother and I were too young. Our grandfather and family friends tried to shield us during recent disasters: the divorce, naturalization, dad's job search. We wanted to believe their assurances, so we folded our panic deep into our suitcases.

An unpaved section of road jarred us from our stupor. We

bounced as our father gripped the steering wheel in surprise. None of us expected dirt roads in America—not in the early nineties, the height of history and progress. Then, a mansion appeared like the ones we'd seen on television, Colonial white with a phalanx of trees on either side. The front door opened and the doctor walked down the driveway to meet us. He and my father hugged and watched with vague disapproval as my brother Tommy and I dragged our luggage to the door. A few minutes later, the doctor's wife came out to help us.

"Prove yourselves," our father said by way of farewell. Then he added in Korean, "Behave or I'll kill you." Once he found stable employment, he could afford to bring over our grandfather, who was subsisting on noodles and broth in an unheated apartment near Busan. My father was a proud man, the eldest son drowning in filial piety. Our grandfather was a patient man except with his own family, and currents of his anger had pulled us into the present situation. Tommy and I could see the tension in my father's neck as he shifted into reverse and backed down the driveway, giving our hosts a terse wave.

The doctor's wife smiled at us as if to say *Everything's fine*, but we knew better. Our father wasn't going far in his search for a new job, but there was something ominous about his departure, as if everyone sensed his journey didn't guarantee success. That unease followed us as we lugged our scuffed vinyl suitcases to the guest room upstairs. Tommy was twelve and I was ten—we were basically human wrecking balls, but I distinctly remember how carefully he avoided banging his suitcase against the walls or scraping them against the hardwood stairs. I trailed behind him, following his lead. Our hosts' names were Paul and Leslie Hrisak, according to the mail in the basket that sat on the bottom swirl of the banister.

We'd met white people in Busan—our father would sometimes bring them over for dinner—but living with them was another matter. These two seemed as odd as their names. After we unpacked, scattering our clothes around the guest room and fighting over who got which identical bed, our hosts called us to the dining room downstairs.

Paul wore a crisp white cotton dress shirt with an orange tie, and Leslie a pastel yellow dress with puffy sleeves. As we passed under the archway into the dining room, the first thing I noticed was the room's dimness: the windows and screen door let in some watery evening light, and wall sconces bearing electric candles were just bright enough to highlight a pair of neatly trussed Cornish hens, which steamed wildly next to Fiestaware bowls heaped with cranberry chutney and peas. Beast that he was, Tommy seemed to take this in stride, but meals in Korea, especially after my parents started sleeping in separate rooms, mostly consisted of sterno-sized offerings of mackerel and pork dumped over rice. On special occasions, dad would serve *budae-jjigae*, a stew consisting of instant noodles, hot dogs, Spam, kimchi, and cheese. He claimed to have invented it, but everyone knew that such an unholy combination could only result from starving Koreans raiding the dumpsters of American military bases after the war. Dad would serve it in our fanciest stone bowls with a bitter cluster of leaves as a garnish.

There were no garnishes, sardonic or otherwise, at the Hrisaks' table. Out of polite efficiency, they had already served us: on my plate were two Medieval-sized dark-meat drumsticks, along with a perfect mound of mashed potatoes holding a dam of gravy. Tommy had a similarly-sized portion—looking back, it was obvious our hosts didn't have children, but as I fidgeted with the cloth napkin on my lap and stared at that plate, it seemed more of a challenge than an offering.

"What's wrong?" Paul said. The lighting emphasized his deep sockets, inset with the bluest eyes I'd ever seen in person. Icy. Even adults who didn't know him as the chief of surgery at Princeton General became self-conscious about their posture and grammar around him, though retirement seemed to have left him with slower vowels and a barely perceptible slouch. Leslie's posture was impeccable and persistent, as if it were part of a job she'd never retire from.

"I think they're just tired," she said. "Right, boys?"

Tommy and I were both good Korean Presbyterians—the same way decorum had been instilled in our hosts, religion had been beaten into us. We waited with our heads bowed, breathing in the fog of poultry as the gravy on our plates congealed.

"Let's begin, shall we?" Paul said, passing his wife a bowl of carrots.

And just like that, without grace but with a certain American grace—a blustery dedication to forging ahead—our first real meal in this new country commenced.

After dinner, Tommy and I bolted upstairs, leaving the Hrisaks to clean up the leftovers and make some recalculations about portion sizes. Over the next few days, we adjusted to each other quickly, the Hrisaks bending their routines and giving us space as we reverted to our natural states. I filched like a magpie while our hosts worked side by side to prepare meals and scrub our muddy handprints off the walls. On our fourth night in their mansion, I emptied my pockets onto the bedsheet. I'd collected a #1 Ticonderoga pencil, some photographs, heart-shaped paperclips, a black marble. The thievery was thrilling enough, but as I mentally catalogued the items, I got the sense that the photographs weren't merely trinkets—their combination of paper, gloss, and image held some deep revelation. Who were these strange Americans we were living with?

It would be a long night. My brother was sitting cross-legged and gawking at the nude tribeswomen in one of Paul's *National Geographic* magazines. Tommy had a bowl of popcorn which he occasionally lifted to his mouth like a horse gumming oats from a bucket. His focus on these tasks meant peace, for the moment.

The first photograph came from Paul's office, frame and all: it was a shot of the doctor holding me when I was maybe four years old. He was wearing a suit with a wide lemon-yellow tie and had just tossed me high into the air. We were maybe at a park, a field of tall grass in the background. He was visiting Busan as part of a university exchange program; my father served as his guide and interpreter. Paul was pale, with white hair, even then. He wasn't a tall man, but he was blessed with the face of an American aristocrat—imagine the captain of Yale's lacrosse team at his 40th class reunion. In the photo, he was laughing, his attentive gaze fixed on the amazing flying boy.

A few other pictures popped out when I slid open the frame, mostly old people I didn't recognize. One was a Polaroid, presumably some distant Hrisak relative. The face was marred by fingerprints now permanently burned into the paper, but it belonged to an elderly white man with fierce bushy eyebrows. The lens had focused on his open mouth, bellowing at the height of some electric madness. I leaned the photo against the lamp on my nightstand and let him face the window. His silent scream joined feathery insect sounds and peeper frogs, a desperate struggle for survival against the matte black outside.

The Bakelite flip clock read 10:50 p.m. "Hey fatty." My brother had silently moved to stand next to my bed. "Where did you get those from?" he said, jerking his chin towards my treasures. He was about a foot taller but slim, a sinewy mass of twitching muscles. We were dressed nicely enough in denim shorts and pastel polo shirts, but we both had the same unfortunate haircuts. The most popular style at the time was a crew cut plus a rat tail, but the haircuts we were permitted were more like flattops, which we maintained with a waxy hair gel. Our first night in the mansion, Tommy discovered the gel was flammable: I woke to see a glowing orange disk glide under me and hit the wall. We scrambled under the bed and extinguished the flames just in time.

I slid the stack of photographs behind me. "The doctor's wife gave them to me," I said.

"You're a freaking liar," he shot back, shining a flashlight in my eyes. I squinted, suddenly tired. The flashlight clicked off and he vanished, replaced by a reddish afterimage and a stabbing pain. "The doctor's gonna find out," he said, his voice ominous as the room's colors strained and settled like a developing photograph.

"You're gonna tell?"

"Doctor's gonna find out."

"Gonna tattle?"

"You're done for," he kept saying.

"Tattle tale tit . . ." I'd overheard neighborhood kids scream-chanting this rhyme.

"Shut up now. I'm going to bed," he said.

"Went and had a fit—" He threw the entire bowl of popcorn, which landed on my bedspread, kernels mixing in with my artifacts. "Damn it," I said, hopping to the floor.

"Serves you right, thief." He pulled the covers over his face.

I brushed away the popcorn and rearranged the photographs. I had to rely on moonlight, which meant standing in front of the window, which was locked open to let the late summer breeze in. I worked quickly, aware that a thin screen was the only protection from scissor-faced insects and other nighttime horrors. There was a shrieking noise and wind chimes—Tommy said no, he couldn't hear anything. "And shut up, too." From outside, a crashing sound and a booming, disembodied voice sent me scrambling to bed, the thin bedsheet fluttering hot and wet over my face.

It was around nine a.m. when the curtains parted with the snap of sparrow wings and the room burst with light. "Dr. Hrisak wants you up for chores," Leslie said, patting my arm. I suspected they referred to each other as "Dr. Hrisak" and "Mrs. Hrisak" even when we weren't around. We thought they were odd, but it was easier to follow their directions—don't curse, don't bring animals inside, wear shirts to the dinner table, and we mostly obeyed.

I stomped down the wooden stairs and slumped over the table. Leslie sat beside me, peering over horn-rimmed reading glasses at *The New York Times* as I ate my cereal slowly, stalling, until the doctor walked in. He sat across from me and placed a napkin on his lap, even though he wasn't eating.

Paul was in his sixties and hard of hearing. Raising our voices to adults was as unthinkable as calling them by their first names— we didn't like repeating ourselves, and we'd shy away when moved closer to hear better. It was easier to avoid him, and there were so many distractions: wrestling in the backyard, trying to shove each other in the pond, and accompanying Leslie on trips to the grocery store. This particular morning, she must have insisted on some meaningful interaction between the men in the house. The Hrisaks were hosting their annual summer party that week, so our job was to beautify the grounds by pulling weeds. The garden was surrounded by a chain-link fence to thwart deer, with a path through the middle made of rotting boards. Paul looked strangely underdressed in cargo shorts and a white tank top. It was already unbearably hot, the insects flying into our hair, sleeves, ears. I wiped the sweat from my forehead and pulled at a dandelion, but the stem broke off and the root remained in the soil. Shrugging, I tossed the leaves in the bucket. The doctor saved the finest tomatoes in a plastic Cool Whip container. The rest he mashed into the dirt with his foot.

"There's a beast in here," Tommy said, holding up a small brown frog. He bounced it a few times in his hand.

With some effort, Paul stood up and walked over. "That's a toad. *Bufo americanus.* A native of the New World and of course plentiful here in Princeton." At times like these, he spoke as if addressing a note-taking class of lesser surgeons. "There has been talk of changing the nomenclature." He laughed to himself. "And perhaps they will. Simpler language for a simpler era."

"We need a hero to slay this beast," Tommy said. He turned it over and stabbed at it with his finger.

"The only beast to be slain here is indolence," declared Paul.

"Hey Jason, you want to take a picture?"

"I do not," I said, glaring at my brother.

"Jason's a photographer. A idealogerrr. He takes pictures," Tommy said in a singsong voice, emphasizing the word *takes*. After a windup, he pretended to pitch the toad to me and I flinched. I gave him a look that said, *You got me, OK, now stop.* The doctor kneeled and frowned at a tomato plant, fussing with its leaves.

I launched a dirt clod square at Tommy's chest, but it hit him in the neck, a spray of dirt flying into his nose and eyes. He snorted and stamped like a brain-damaged bull, then scoured the ground for rocks.

"Enough," Paul warned.

"Did Jason tell you about his collection?" Tommy asked, brushing off his shirt.

"Tell the doctor what you've been doing with his magazines," I screamed, pointing at Tommy. "And why you stole those photographs and hid them under my bed." Tommy's face reddened. He threw his bucket across the garden, opened his mouth to scream, and abruptly collapsed. The toad flung itself from his hand as the doctor sprinted over. In his last seconds of consciousness, Tommy was laid over the doctor's lap like the Pieta, his eyes wide, mouth open as if chewing on a gigantic question. He reached out for me, and that gesture shocked me even more than his face. I stood frozen for a few seconds before remembering to grab his hand. By then, the doctor was shouting at me, and my brother's eyes were closed.

"Get help," Paul repeated. I ran into the house without a word. It must have looked like I was going to call Leslie, or the hospital.

Really, I was sprinting upstairs to our bedroom to hide the evidence, that black-magic photograph I'd snuck under Tommy's pillow—which had, for all I knew, just killed him.

Tommy survived his brush with the dark arts. He'd actually had a panic attack and fainted. If I'd arranged my curses just right, perhaps he would have turned into a toad. Or we could have switched places: he'd be the fat kleptomaniac and I'd be the expert at making fart noises with my hands. That evening, our dad called. Wherever he was, there was a symphony of noise in the background. I pictured a diner, complete with dinging bells and clattering plates. The classifieds were spread in front of him, opportunity after opportunity circled and crossed out. "All is well—that's what everyone says. Tell the truth about your brother," he demanded. I looked around the kitchen for help but found none.

"All *is* well," I replied, quickly passing the phone back to Tommy, who smirked down at me from a tall stool and swung his legs to kick my chair. In front of him was a wooden bowl of cherry tomatoes. He made a whistling noise as he tossed one in the air and caught it in his mouth. "Anxiety" was the diagnosis from the hospital. The doctors recommended rest in a calm environment for the next few days. His face broad and innocent, Tommy asked when he could return to his work in the garden.

Even though Paul wanted me to continue weeding, Leslie intervened and said we brothers should spend some time together. So there we were, facing each other at the thick oak kitchen table.

Tommy picked up the heavy magnifying glass Paul used to read the newspaper and examined me through it. "Dad said only room in the new house for the eldest," he said, blinking a gigantic bloodshot eye.

"Liar."

"And he's gonna get me a freaking wheelchair 'cause of all my anxieties. And then I'm gonna run your fat ass over with it."

"Hardly," I said, looking down at my lap. I flipped through *The New York Times* on the table, searching for the funny pages.

"You're gonna live in the forest and eat toads. *Buffoonus americanos*. But someday, a toad will eat *you*."

"Shut up . . . hospital boy," I said. It felt cheap and mean, but I didn't take it back.

"Dad said he's coming back for me next week. Maybe no one's coming for you," he said, standing to examine a family of wooden elephants displayed on the bookshelf behind us. He walked out of the room, leaving me to ponder the very real possibility that even the doctor and his wife might vanish and the fruit in the bowls on the table would rot and I would wait there forever.

The next week, Tommy took his revenge. After all, he'd fainted like a character in a Victorian novel—in front of our host, no less. Also, he'd begged me with his eyes, and all I'd given was a horrified stare. I picked out the rocks he snuck into my food and didn't tell anyone when I woke to find him putting my hand in a bowl of warm pond water. I think it was water, anyway. But as the week went on, and my sympathy dwindled, I began plotting.

• • •

It happened when we were in Paul's study, playing a game he'd just invented: whoever went the longest without speaking would win a little metal penlight that vaguely resembled a lightsaber. After a period of silent taunting, we opted to ignore each other. Tommy stood on a chair, trying to reach the anatomy books at the top of the shelves. I stared out the window at the forest outside, reviewing my strategy. The doctor was somewhere upstairs.

I didn't have anything to lose. There were two doors to the study, and since Paul was upstairs, he'd have to come through the closed door nearest us. It was perfect. I strolled over to the desk and unearthed a cigar box which was mostly hidden by a stack of magazines. Now I had Tommy's attention. I slid a cigar from the box and with some effort bit off the tip, like I'd seen in a cartoon. I spit the tobacco into the wastebasket and wiped my mouth. There was a Zippo in the desk drawer and I flicked it open. *What the frig are you doing?* Tommy whispered. A few moments later, I heard Paul creaking slowly down the stairs on his bad knees. But Tommy didn't seem to care. He kept flapping his hands in excitement. After I held a finger to my lips, he sat down, mesmerized. Usually, he was the daring and impulsive one. I ran the cigar under my nose, relishing the freshness of the experience, along with the exotic scent. I grabbed a lighter and the cigar crackled over the flame. *My insane little brother,* Tommy mouthed. He was immensely proud of me, even if pride was only one of several emotions he was trying to contain. I closed my eyes like a jazz saxophonist and placed the cigar between my lips.

"What's going on in there?" came Paul's voice. He must have smelled it and was now really hoofing it across the hall. I raised my eyebrows and took another puff. My brother looked at the door, then at me. The moment the door handle turned, I tossed the burning cigar into my brother's lap and bolted through the empty door.

●　●　●

Leslie drove a purple sedan. Normally, I would have been embarrassed to ride in such a girly-colored vehicle, but today I sat with my back straight, taking in the world from the backseat. A tuft of Paul's white hair rose above his headrest like a cloud. I loved my new flashlight but couldn't see the beam in the sunlight, so I pressed my forehead to the cool window and watched the scenery.

She steered through a grid of mansions and thick trees. "There's Einstein's old home," she said, slowing as we passed a little white house with a big porch. It was too small and plain, I decided, searching instead for a solid-gold palace shaped like a mushroom cloud. We turned the corner and Paul pointed to a baseball field. He began to ask a question but caught himself.

"You don't play baseball, do you?" he asked. I said no, that was my brother. I could barely walk up a flight of stairs without panting. Tommy was rotting at home doing his punishment—I couldn't wait to tell him about this drive. The air smelled like freshly mowed grass and someone was burning a woodpile in a distant backyard. Paul closed his eyes again. I rolled down the window and let the wind tug at my fingers.

It was around noon and the sun would have been a problem anywhere else. But this was Princeton, where the surfaces were ancient. The town absorbed rather than reflected the light, and there was a softness to the old houses, like the smoothest sea glass or worn pages of a book.

Scattered mansions gave way to green fields, streaks of yellow wheat at the borders. Leslie drove a few miles on a rutted dirt road. "We used to buy all our veggies here when I was a girl," she said as the air got dustier. She had mannish short hair and was wearing a pink dress with white flowers on it. At the farm, Paul gave me money and let me pay for the vegetables—the responsibility was part of my reward, he said.

We took a different route home. The scenery was almost enough for me to forget about my father's job search. He'd been gone over a week, during which we'd almost burned down the Hrisak's house and forced an emergency room visit. Our grandfather was still stranded in Korea, but Leslie's purple car outpaced those worries. Out the window were scenes I'd only seen on TV. Without even trying, I'd discovered the peace and harmony my father was ultimately searching for.

After carrying the corn, squash, and other veggies to the kitchen, I checked on Tommy, who glared up at me, then turned back to his essay on integrity and honesty. In the margin, he wrote, *I'm going to frigging kill you you turkey turd burger.* Like a TV cop during a traffic stop, I clicked on the flashlight and aimed the beam at his eyes.

Later that day, Leslie consolidated boxes in the attic. Hoping to find more baubles and trinkets, I volunteered to help. In a few hours, at the opposite end of the attic, there were only cobweb-shadows over a wide patch of floorboards. Dust floated in the sunlight, creating a haze—if I squinted, it seemed like the boxes were simply evaporating.

She wore a purple bandanna, and from pictures I'd seen, she didn't look much older than she had on her wedding day. Her hair was long hair then, down to her waist. She was a small woman. I could see it in her wrists and fingers as she lifted wine glasses to the light. They had a date etched on the bowl, but before I could read it, she wrapped them in brown paper and set them in a smaller box. Watching her repeat this simple action, I forgot about my father for a while. But he surfaced again as we slid the packed box across the room. "What happens when my father comes back?" I asked, meaning, *What happens if he can't find a job or can only afford to take one of us with him?*

"Well," she answered carefully, "the paperwork's finished, so once he's employed, he'll bring your grandfather over from Korea. And you'll all move in together, I suppose." I'd almost expected her to say, *I know you don't like your family. If you want, you can move in with us.* But it was impossible—Princeton was too foreign, too old, too fragile for someone like me. Leslie stood over me, then grabbed my hands. Without thinking, I held on and let her pull me to my feet. "We're having a party tomorrow," she said. "Let's forget everything else, shall we?"

We spent the rest of the afternoon shucking corn. After we finished, I retreated to the living room to slouch in my favorite chair. It faced a brass bowl filled with dusty firewood, placed where a TV should have been. When cars passed in front of the windows, its seams and dents shifted. I watched, idly speculating about all the millionaires driving past. The drapes were porous, the outside world blissfully muted.

On the wall above my chair hung a red-and-white rug depicting rows of alien-like stick figures holding hands. The carpet was light brown. There were magazines on the coffee table, but they were filled with big words and tedious charts. Aside from the brass bowl, the only interesting object in the room was a flea trap, a glowing bulb above a tray of sticky paper. A few unlucky fleas and beetles twitched on it, their free legs waving.

Tommy entered the room with a bored, predatory look in his eyes. He glanced at the flea trap, then at me. I left quickly.

In the living room, I could pretend to read magazines, but it would only be a matter of time before Paul spotted me wandering and assigned a chore. I considered my options and headed right into the lion's den.

"Bored?" he asked, looking up from his desk. I shook my head. He laughed. "Of course not." I stared at the cigar-sized hole burned into the carpet.

"Tommy wanted to know if there were chores he could do," I said.

"Tommy said that, did he? What a thoughtful brother you are."

I backed away slowly, realizing I didn't have much of a plan now that I was in the doctor's study. My new plan was to back out of the room. "Work is . . . important for a man," he said finally. "It's a shame I don't have anything for you."

My eyes fixed on a blue-and-white striped bowl at the top of a display cabinet. It was about the size of a salad bowl. There were more colorful pieces surrounding it, but they didn't hold my attention. "You like pottery?" Paul asked, as if he were about to offer a gift. I nodded. "You have good taste," he said, walking over to the cabinet. He lifted the bowl from its stand and shook a dead spider from it. "This might well be the capstone of my collection. Anasazi." He raised his voice as he switched into teaching mode. "The Anasazi were American Indians who lived in the Mesa Verde, near New Mexico. Leslie attended college there. The best archeological minds are still trying to figure out how these people lived, considering the lack of vegetation in the area. No one knows where they buried their dead. They've unearthed small burial sites but not enough for such a large settlement. There were cliff dwellings—have you learned about this in school yet?" I shook my head. "The Anasazi are also notable because one day they simply . . ." He held his hand out in a fist, tightened and opened it, shaking particles of nothing onto the carpet.

"Vanished?" I said.

"About the same time this bowl was made, actually. 1100 AD."

"And they just left that behind?" I asked.

"Among other artifacts."

"Why did they vanish?"

"Ah. Another mystery. Some scholars believe there was a drought. Or disease. Some . . . intrepid explorer recently found evidence of cannibalism among the tribe. This . . . claim could always be fiction, something to scare up grant money."

"Cannibals." This wasn't history. It couldn't be. The ground under my feet never felt solid, but I'd never imagined entire tribes of people could disappear overnight.

"They left behind carvings, but no one can decipher them. I've come to believe this bowl came from a dubious source," he said, holding it so I could see the pattern inside. Four pencil-thin blue stripes curved toward a vanishing point in the center. It certainly didn't look more than eight hundred years old, but the pattern was impeccable, the lines so straight it was hard to imagine they'd been painted by a human hand. I was suddenly impatient to hold it, to trace my fingers along its pale slopes.

"This may be the only surviving spirit bowl. Usually when the craftsman died, his kinsmen smashed the bowl to set his spirit free. Dubious, as I said, that this one is still intact. The man I bought it from has since gone the way of the Anasazi, so to speak." He laughed.

"Can I hold it?" I asked.

With some effort, he put the bowl back on its stand in the cabinet.

Tommy strode into the room. "What's shakin'?" he said. I wasn't about to give away my new secret, but I couldn't think of a distraction. I'd need Paul to play along, too.

"Come help me set the table," Leslie called to us from down the hall.

During the party, I snuck down to the basement and stole a bottle of port, mostly because I'd admired its crystal decanter. I really began to covet it when Paul noticed my interest and moved it atop the liquor cabinet, but it was easily reachable by standing on a chair. Like I said, the Hrisaks didn't have kids.

I switched on the fluorescent magnifying light above the desk Paul used to tie flies, revealing stacks of clear plastic containers filled with feathery objects and metal tools. If my father didn't return, I could be an assistant. Paul could say, "Tweezer-thingy," and I would place it in his palm. I took a sip of the port and tried to keep a straight face. My mouth burned as I swallowed, my throat convulsing against the liquid. *This stuff's gone bad*, I thought. But I'd already made the effort to get the bottle, so I had to follow through. I took a less enthusiastic sip, listening to the party above. I could make out the light classical music wafting through the cherrywood speakers. I sat at the desk and loosened my tie, pressing my back against the chair. Tommy would be too busy charming the other guests to notice my absence. But the doctor wouldn't. I walked up the stairs, feeling queasy.

While the basement had been cool and smelled like dry wood with a whiff of ancient motor oil, the first floor was oppressively humid, the air a clash of perfumes and sweat. A bald man carrying a stock pot full of steaming corn speed-walked past me in the hall. The loud conversations and symphony music drove me from room to room. Inside Paul's study, a white bowl warming under halogen display lights quietly waited for me, but this evening, the door was locked. I put my ear to the door and heard a faint humming, as if people inside were having a hushed argument. A passing party guest shot me a disapproving look and I reluctantly left.

There were enough people that no one really noticed me. Some waved or tried to introduce themselves, but I just nodded and walked on like I was looking for something. By this point, I felt the liquor in my brain, and I had to concentrate to keep from stumbling. Color swirled around me, the pinks and yellows of the women's late-summer dresses.

I drifted, at the mercy of gravity and my own tired legs. Tommy was holding a snifter of grape juice, chatting with some older men. "Here's my little brother," he said, grabbing me by the shoulders. I shook free with porcine grace and fled the room. It felt like a liquid weight was coalescing in my head, weighing it down, and my neck strained to carry it. *Left foot, right, neck straight, don't panic*, I repeated to myself.

The anticipation, the crowd, the music—it all told me this party was supposed to be my first step into the adult world, but I'd screwed it up. My drunken stumbling would lead to prolonged stumbling through the years to come, and there was nothing I could to about it.

I found myself on the back porch, gripping the edge of a picnic table to remain upright. The cool breeze licked at my eyeballs as I watched the crowd inside the house through the screen door. Inside, Paul rarely paused to chat, though the guests waved and shook his hand as he passed. He was smiling, or at least doing his best. He slid open the screen door and sat across from me without saying a word. Looking back, I think he was about to ask whether I was having fun, but the answer must have been clear. There were a couple of smokers outside, but they didn't notice us. The breeze already a distant memory, humidity crept beneath my shirt. I loosened my tie again and sat on my hands, pressing them against the slats in the bench. Paul sighed and stood up slowly, trying to hide the pain in his knees. As he passed, he put his hand on my shoulder as if to say, *I know how you feel*, then returned to the crowd.

Tommy was too busy entertaining guests to remember that *we* were guests, but I knew we didn't belong and wouldn't stay much longer. Somewhere in the wilds of New Jersey, our father's search was drawing to a close. Even if he didn't find a job, Tommy and I couldn't stay in this moneyed purgatory forever.

I'd been lying in the warm grass for hours, maybe, when someone lifted and carried me into the house.

"Are you a cannibal?" I asked. The man shifted me in his arms and I heard Paul's voice.

"Truly your father's son. I hope you remember this."

I said something like, "Please don't kill me," and may have offered up my brother as an alternative. But beyond this easy betrayal, I didn't say much. The trip to my room must have taken just a few minutes.

"Damn, you're heavy," Paul said. His knees popped as he set me down on the bed. Shrill insect noises floated through the window. He put his hand on my forehead. It was huge and cold and after a few seconds everything went quiet. The sickness and tension flowed away—only calm and sleep remained.

"Left foot, right foot, head straight, don't panic," I mumbled, out of habit. He laughed quietly and left. After he flicked off the light, the room was still faintly illuminated by the tiki lights near the deck. Tommy must have been outside chatting with guests because his laughter, careless and loud, drifted up through the window.

I woke around six a.m. with a slight headache. The inside of my mouth tasted like a carcass soaked in methanol. From what I'd seen in movies, I'd expected a blinding hangover. I poured myself some cereal. It was nice eating alone. I could sit and think all I wanted without interruption. As the sun rose, I worked a little in the garden. I knew some kind of Old Testament punishment was coming but somehow wasn't worried. I'd survived the party and that was enough. No one mentioned anything at lunch and I considered the possibility that my drunkenness at the party went unnoticed. I slumped on a leather recliner in the living room, guilt sharpening my senses—upstairs, Leslie sorted through what seemed like centuries of memorabilia in the attic, throwing away so much. The doctor held court in the garden, holding tomatoes to the sky and lecturing to an invisible class. Tommy threw rocks at ducks in the pond and did pushups until he puked. None of this was unusual that summer, but now I could see the true shape of things, trace the outlines of each sad world.

My grandfather called, ostensibly to see how we were, and there was a loud buzz on the telephone line. Paul frowned when I answered our grandfather's questions in Korean, so I switched to English. "How is America?" he asked. He was really asking, *When can I join you?* His voice was tight, but only I could hear. He asked about my grades and my father, and I replied, "Grades perfect, father good," both of which were lies, since it was summer and I hadn't heard from dad in four days. "We're having big fun here," I said, handing off the phone to Paul and leaving my grandfather to wonder why I'd started talking like a B-movie Indian. "Heap big trouble" pretty accurately describes what I was carrying on my shoulders. It felt like the low hum from that long distance call never quite left my ears.

International calls were expensive back then, but maybe our grandfather's was worth it, since it expedited my father's search—or maybe Paul let slip that that during our dad's two-week absence, his 12 year-old had to be rushed to the ER and his 10 year-old had gotten drunk. The night before my father arrived, Tommy and I pretended to clean while the Hrisaks actually cleaned. Dad would arrive in time for dinner and would share his news then. "Everything would work out." The Hrisaks seemed to genuinely believe this. My family knew it wasn't true: we'd fled a nation that was ripped in half—and we were from the good half. That night, the doctor's study was unlocked. Realizing it might be my last chance, I touched the spirit bowl and instantly regretted it. The blue lines, slightly indented, were spaced as far apart as my fingers. The surface was slightly damp, and the whole bowl vibrated quietly. When I managed to set it back into the cabinet, my hands continued its trembling.

Dinner the next day. I watched my father eat, my chubby hands gripping the table. Something had been welling in my chest for the past week. "Everything will work out" didn't change the fact that my father had returned with bad posture and a flat, joyless smile. How many people in New Jersey needed Korean interpreters? My chest tightened and I could hardly breathe as dad cleared his throat and stood. Everyone else waited calmly. I took a few breaths, drawing nothing. My heart pounded in my ears, and I scrambled from the room.

In the doctor's study, I stopped in front of the cabinet to catch my breath. Everyone else had shaken off their surprise and started to follow me, but I didn't care. I stood on the bottom shelf and grabbed it, the heat and glory of the bowl cradled in my hands.

"What do you have there, Jason?" my father said. Apparently he didn't know anything about pottery. Maybe he thought I was hungry and wanted cereal. "Where you going, tiger?" he asked as I exited the room. *Tie-guh.*

"Oh my God," Paul began. "Jason—"

I ran through the kitchen, pushing their hands away. Now came the real yelling and commotion. "He's lost it. Call a SWAT team," Tommy yelled. Because Princeton had lots of those.

Upstairs, in our bedroom, I scrambled out the open window, onto the gable, balancing myself with a leg on either side. It was starting to get dark out; the grass below was indigo. The stars emerged in constellations I'd never seen before. I held the bowl in both hands and caught my breath, greedily sucking in the night air.

"He's here," Leslie said. She took a step into my room. "What are you doing with that, darling?" My father jogged a little as he approached the window.

"Snipers," Tommy suggested.

That's me on the roof. I've summited Mount Princeton and know exactly what I'm doing. The bowl is between my sweating hands—it's charged somehow, the current shaking my heart until all I hear is the rush of my blood. I can see my family though the bedroom window, advancing. My feet slip a little on the shingles as

I back away towards the gutter. Everything stops except the ringing in my ears. And as the world leans toward this rooftop in Princeton, anticipating my next move, I hurl down the bowl and it smashes with a crisp rattling sound, the pieces cascading onto the lawn below. The universe exhales. Then my foot slips, my leg following, and then my chest slams against the roof, my fingers scraping at the rough shingles as gravity takes over.

I don't remember the impact, or much until the hospital. In the waiting room, my father made his announcement: he'd used his connections to secure a job at a university near Toledo. The doctors made their own announcement to the family: I had a couple bruised ribs and a broken wrist. Later that evening, my father made me haul my luggage from the Hrisaks to his car, my hospital bracelet flapping as I dragged my suitcase with one hand. Paul stayed inside, but Leslie emerged and waved as we pulled out of the driveway. I was the only one who spotted her in time to return the farewell.

The drive to Ohio reminds me of my relationship with my father, and my life in general: a winding, fevered glide punctuated by my father demanding "Why?" *What the fuck is wrong with you?* He'd been asking since the hospital, and I still didn't have an answer. The first few times, he actually turned to face me.

I still didn't have an answer days later, after my father maneuvered the car through a small development of nearly-identical single-story houses, each with green vinyl siding. It was late evening, and the road was freshly paved, the sidewalks lined with

Maidenhair saplings. Instinctively, I knew one of these houses was ours. In Busan, we lived in the shadow of the mountains. There was a flatness to this American neighborhood that extended to the crew-cut lawns, the grimly efficient symmetry of the cul-de-sac's layout. "This was supposed to be a surprise," our father grumbled as he pulled in front of a house.

"What?" Tommy whined, sounding like he'd just woken up. The front door flew open and in the doorway stood the silhouette of my grandfather. Even from the car, I recognized the slight stoop, hands behind his back in a vaguely martial pose. I could picture his gray stubble, his eyes shut into neat little arches as he flashed a smile. Life in postwar Korea had left him with teeth like Indian corn, but in moments like these, he didn't care who saw. He flicked on the porch light and waved to us, beckoning. He didn't know I was in a cast, or that my father was stewing in a brine of shame and confusion over his strained relationship with Paul. I realized my father meant this moment was supposed to be a *happy* surprise. He probably thought I'd ruined it.

Maybe I had—in some ways, I never left that rooftop in Princeton. Even now, I can picture the curve of that white bowl, the way it rested in my hands, begging for me to curl my fingers around the rim and slam my palms together. Smashing it brought holy silence, but I didn't consider the cost. Even as my father switched off the engine and the headlights winked out, I sat listening to the tick of the engine. My grandfather was smiling because he believed he could start anew, buoyed by the hot blood of his grandsons and the piety of his son. I wondered if the spirit I'd released by smashing the bowl would follow us across this new threshold. None of us could yet make sense of what happened in New Jersey, but I couldn't shake the notion that our time in Princeton revealed how little we understood or even liked each other. We were, in fact, broken beyond repair. As I opened the door and stepped from the car, my cast glowing in the streetlight, I wondered if we'd spend the rest of our lives gathering up the shards.

NOAH ALVAREZ is a Cuban-American author from Lexington, Kentucky. He has published two short stories and is working on his debut novel. You can find Noah's work in *Cutleaf Journal* and *Shotgun Honey*. He currently lives in North Carolina with his wife and daughter.

My uncle Rick died when I was in high school from liver failure. Despite recovering from alcoholism and achieving sobriety, the damage to his liver had already been done, and he passed away as the next person on the list to receive a transplant. At the time of his death I was young and I tried to run away from the emotional impact of his sudden death, so it was something I blocked out for a few years.

There's no specific moment when it all came to fruition, but rather something that slowly poured out of me. I'm proud to have represented him in my first published story.

VICTORIA BALLESTEROS is a writer from California. The youngest of nine children, she is the daughter and sister of immigrants whose work is inspired by her bicultural upbringing. Her work has appeared in *Cutleaf Journal, trampset, Your Impossible Voice,* and *Best Small Fictions* 2024. She is enrolled in the creative writing program at UCLA extension.

My mother sacrificed so much of herself as a wife and mother, and that influenced my own rejection of the cultural and societal dynamics which expected her to do that. I wanted to capture some of that in a story. There are also bits and pieces of my childhood woven throughout. For example, the house where I grew up was across the street from the freeway, and we often had kids from the neighborhood dropping in for my Mamá's cooking.

EXODUS OKTAVIA BROWNLOW is a writer, sewist, author, and editor native to Blackhawk, Mississippi. She is a graduate of Mississippi Valley State University with a BA in English, and Mississippi University for Women with an MFA in creative writing. She is an associate editor at *Fractured Lit* and is the editor in chief of *The Loveliest Review*. Exodus has been published or has forthcoming work with *Electric Literature*, *West Branch*, *Denver Quarterly*, *F(r)iction*, *BOOTH*, *CRAFT*, and more. She has work featured in *Best Microfiction 2021* and *2022*. Her piece "The Terrible Darling" was featured as a *Wigleaf Top 50* 2022 selection. Exodus's essay "When the World Was Ending We Wore the Cornrows. We Twisted Our Coils, and We Waited." was selected for *Best American Essays 2024* as notable. Find her on Instagram @ CooCoo4AfroPuffs and at exodusoktaviabrownlow.com. Her favorite color is green.

I am the eldest daughter out of three siblings. Being the eldest often means you get to receive your first taste of mama'ing, of parenting, pretty soon and more so than your siblings ever will. When I wrote this story, I was creating from a space that sought to give grace to parents, and especially to mamas, who at one point had only the whole of themselves (and potentially their partners) to consider, and in an instant poured through the sift of hours upon hours, had the whole of another to consider, a newborn baby. If parenting is a practice, and it is, if mama'ing is a practice, and it is—how may the craft of its execution be refined over time? The eldest child, being a kind of rough draft. The youngest, receiving the most skilled mama'ing of all. And that in itself, that refined skill, only obtained through the demands of time, through deeply unfair and deeply beautiful human experiences, through the balancing act of a mother becoming who she is and needs to be, alongside who her children are dreaming to be.

C. G. CRAWFORD is an MFA student in Creative Writing at the University of Alabama. He is from Birmingham, Alabama, but he calls home the place of his maternal roots in the rural parts of West Alabama. He received a Master of Theological Studies from Vanderbilt University. He was a 2022 Roots. Wounds. & Words. (RWW) Storytellers of Color Fiction Fellow, and he has published works with *al.com, Faithfully Magazine,* and *THE WITNESS.* He is currently working on several short stories, novels, and plays that wrestle with the soul, the surreal, and the South in ways that give shape to a collective human experience.

"Wild Hogs on the Backside of Yonder" came about in thought of African American history and land ownership. It is the story of a man fighting to defend his land in the face of a white land-owning family (the

McGrangers) seeking to take his land for their own special interests. If you know stories like that of Macon Dead I in Toni Morrison's *Song of Solomon,* then you will know River's story too. Despite the McGrangers's intimidation tactics to get him to sell his land, River and his small community of friends will do everything in their power to defend his land at all costs.

I wrote this story with my grandfather in mind. He has had to deal with his own battles over land ownership in rural Alabama, including tactics by his own neighbors. Once upon a time, there was a fight over one small little corner of his land. The fight took place in the court and between two of his cornfields that are split between the rocky gravel road that leads to his house. I thought about my grandfather's story, and the stories of other people who have had to fight for their land through the court – and through blood. You've got the Hatfields and the McCoys in the Appalachian. You've got the Duttons of Yellowstone. And then you've got the forgotten, ignored, and often untold Black and indigenous people's stories, in the South and beyond, who have had to defend the land that runs through their blood until their very last breath. "Wild Hogs on the Backside of Yonder" is a part of the latter. It blends fact and fiction to tell of a historical truth. A truth that needs to be remembered, recognized, and repeated so that, even in fiction, we never forget what has been stolen, and we, whoever the "we" may be, find a way to ensure that folks like River are never forgotten – from the living to the dead.

MONIC DUCTAN is the author of *Daughters of Muscadine*, a short story collection about working-class families in rural Georgia. *Muscadine* won both the Weatherford Award for Appalachian fiction and the Tennessee Book Award in fiction. Monic won a 2023 Tennessee Arts Commission grant for fiction, and her prose has appeared in *Oxford American*, *Appalachian Review*, *South Carolina Review*, and elsewhere. She's also the poetry winner of the 2025 Tennessee Williams & New Orleans Literary Festival contest for her poem,

"Mama Took Grandma to Vote for Kennedy." She teaches at Tennessee Tech University.

This story came about because I was reflecting on an incident near my home in Tennessee. I saw two boys who looked like they'd been fighting. It upset me to see that the smaller one was likely being bullied. I pulled over to ask if he needed help. While my personal story didn't go the way of my fictional version of the account, I still felt compelled to write a creative version of what happened. I invented a backstory for the bullied boy, and I created an older woman narrator who tries to help the boy.

LATANYA MCQUEEN is the author of two books—the essay collection *And It Begins Like This* (Black Lawrence Press, 2017) and the novel *When the Reckoning Comes* (Harper Perennial, 2021; Olive Editions 2024), a Goodreads Choice nominee and Bram Stoker Award finalist. She is an Assistant Professor of English at NC State and teaches in their MFA program.

I lived in Missouri for several years

and during my time there, I learned about the popularity of American Civil War Reenactments. Within the United States, they are one of the most popular hobbies. While they largely originated in part to upload the Old South myth, in recent years authenticity is the guiding aesthetic and principle among some groups of Civil War Reenactment enthusiasts. These reenactors aim to be as historically accurate as possible, striving for the authentic replication of the Civil War soldier experience.

I've always been interested in how people interpret history, in the way we pick and choose what to remember, along with how some aspects of history often get revised or erased. A lot of my writing, both then and since, deals with the relationship between the past and our present moment—how has the past continued to define and shape how we see ourselves? With "Middling" I wanted to explore these concerns through the lens of this interracial couple. Both of these characters have a very different relationship to the history of the Civil War, and when one becomes obsessed with re-enactments as a means to connect to his own ancestry, it forces a reevaluation not just of how each of them has understood the past, but also in how they've come to see and understand their relation and each other.

JENNIFER MORALES is a poet, fiction writer, and performance artist based in rural Wisconsin, and a graduate of Antioch University-Los Angeles's MFA program. Their first book, *Meet Me Halfway* (UW Press 2015), a short story collection about life in hyper-segregated Milwaukee, was Wisconsin Center for the Book's 2016 "Book of the Year," among other honors. Other publications include "The Boy Without a Bike," in *Cutting Edge*, edited by Joyce Carol Oates (Akashic 2019) and "The Doorman," in *Fire & Water: Stories from the Anthropocene* (Black Lawrence 2021). Jennifer is a longtime member of the board of the Driftless Writing Center, based in Viroqua, Wisconsin.

"Beantown" is, by far, the most emotionally autobiographical story I've ever written. I say "emotionally" because many of the "factual" bits of the story are false, but the feelings are true. I lived a racially ambiguous childhood in a small Illinois town that was quite literally divided into two sides by railroad tracks. Although our mixed family was Latino, we lived on the Anglo/white side of the tracks, which was deeply puzzling to me as a young child. I knew we kids were perceived as Mexican and "brown" by others in town, yet my mother's light skin and blue eyes gave us some kind of pass, it seemed. After reading "Beantown", my sister Linda reminded me that the name the Anglos gave the Mexican part of town was actually "Beanerville" ("beaner" being an anti-Mexican slur)—so look at me, the writer, retroactively granting grace to my racist neighbors with the title of this story!

RUBY HANSEN MURRAY is an award-winning columnist for the *Osage News*, winner of *The Iowa Review* and *Montana Prizes*, and an Indigenous Nations Poets, Tin House, and MacDowell fellow. Find her work in *Cascadia: A Field Guide* (Tupelo Press), *Ecotone, Allotment Stories* (University

of Minnesota Press), *River Mouth Review, Under the Sun, the Massachusetts Review, Pleiades, High Desert Journal, Moss, The Rumpus,* and *Shapes of Native Nonfiction*. She's a citizen of the Osage and Cherokee Nations with West Indian roots, living in the lower Columbia River estuary.

I wrote "There's the Indian" after Ree Drummond began her re-development of downtown Pawhuska, capital of the Osage Reservation. She refurbished an historic mercantile building to sell books and memorabilia popularized by her *Pioneer Woman* blog, a mommy cooking blog replete with photos of the prairie, cowboy and cattle culture in the "middle of nowhere." Drummond married into a ranching family entangled with the Osage as licensed Indian traders and guardians when the Osage were removed from Kansas and sent to the rolling tallgrass prairie in NE Oklahoma. Pawhuska was a dusty, midwestern town with vestiges of the glamour that the oil boom of the 1920s spawned, when Drummond's project began. Multiple developers had hoped to renovate the Triangle Building where an untoward number of lawyers preyed on Osages and their oil wealth over the years, to no avail. Osages were absent from the pages of the Drummond blog and early memoirs. She trafficked in pure cowboy culture/Americana, which is to say, Nature empty of anyone besides the wholesome pioneers of Laura Ingalls Wilder's *Little House on the Prairie*. My protagonist in "There's the Indian" steps out of Osage norms fueled by a desire to make space in the world for his sons.

MICHAEL PACHECO was born in Mexico and raised in the USA. After receiving his Bachelor's Degree from Gonzaga University, he earned his law degree at Willamette University College of Law. He now dedicates his time writing fiction, focusing on literary fiction, speculative fiction and magical realism. Michael now lives in the Sonoran Desert of Arizona. He has been published in forty-three literary journals and magazines in the U.S., Canada, South America, England, and Africa.

This story was inspired by my frequent travels between El Paso, Texas and Tucson, Arizona. Traveling by car gives me the opportunity to enjoy the desert scenery, the mountains, the Joshua trees, the cacti, and the wildlife animals, if you're lucky enough to see them in the daytime. When I see a single farmhouse in the middle of a wheatfield, my mind swirls back to my childhood, where our nearest neighbor was half a mile away. I don't miss the solitude, but I do miss the serenity.

Chicana Feminist and former Rodeo Queen, **TISHA MARIE REICHLE-AGUILERA** (she/her) writes so the desert landscape of her childhood can be heard as loudly as the urban chaos of her adulthood. She is the author of the YA novel, *Breaking Pattern* (Inlandia Books), which received Honorable Mention for First Book of Fiction in English from the International Latino Book Awards, and a prose chapbook, *Stories All Our Own* (Bottlecap Press). Other stories have been anthologized and nominated for awards. She is also a playwright, a Macondista, and works for literary equity through Women Who Submit.

"Beer & Butter Sauce" reflects my obsession with food and my family's love of grandpa's ribs. It is set in the town where my parents grew up, where my life began, in the home of my paternal grandparents. The story was born when I sat down with my students to write about a food item that conjures fond memories but also recalls some kind of tension.

SARP SOZDINLER has been published in *Electric Literature, Kenyon Review, Masters Review, Vol.1 Brooklyn, Normal School,* and *Maudlin House,* among other journals. His stories have been selected or nominated for such anthologies as the Pushcart Prize, Best Small Fictions, and *Wigleaf Top 50*; and shortlisted or selected as a finalist for various literary contests, including the *SmokeLong Quarterly* Grand Micro Prize, *Los Angeles Review* Flash Fiction Award, and the *Passages North's* Waasnode Short Fiction Prize. He is currently at work on his first novel in Philadelphia and Amsterdam.

"Houses Acting Like Cars" began as a meditation on inheritance—not just of blood, but of trauma, memory, and geography. I wanted to explore what it means to grow up surrounded by absence, and how identity often forms in the voids left by other people's choices. Blue emerged from that space, a teenage girl navigating a version of Tampa shaped by contradictions: holy and broken, vibrant and decaying, full of roads that don't quite lead anywhere—kind of like memory, kind of like a dream.

SEJAL SHAH is a writer and educator whose work crosses genres and disciplines. Her story collection, *How to Make Your Mother Cry: fictions* (West Virginia University Press, 2024), includes "Ithaca Is Never Far" and was longlisted for the 2024/2025 Story Prize. Her award-winning essay collection, *This Is One Way to Dance* (University of Georgia Press, 2020), was recommended in the *New York Times,* named a university common read, and an NPR Best Book of the year. Sejal lives outside Rochester, New York; find her online at sejal-shah.com.

"Ithaca Is Never Far" is a retelling of *The Odyssey* from Penelope's point of view. It was also inspired by my experience of growing up and living at some geographic and cultural distance from major metropolitan centers and by the pressure I felt in my twenties to find a partner–especially one who was also of Indian background. When I wrote "Ithaca," I was living in Western Massachusetts, a couple of hours away from Boston. I was struck by a comment I heard from someone I briefly dated who was from Boston that Western Massachusetts (Amherst) was outside of his radius – of where he was willing to travel. I grew up in and outside of Rochester, New York. Western New York is also at some distance (close to six hours) from New York City and Boston. I think places that are at some remove from the bigger cities also have their own culture and sense of place. If someone visits you in Ithaca or in Rochester or in Iowa, it usually means they love you / seeing you is a priority. I was also writing about my frustration at trying to figure out how to find a suitable partner when it seems

the possibilities were somewhat constrained by geography.

When I lived in New York City, I had many visitors who were in New York for something else and visiting me was not the point of their travel; it might have been a side benefit. While my experience in Rochester was not rural, but rather that of growing up in a suburb of a mid-sized city, I later lived in the small city of Decorah, Iowa (population under 8,000), and while there and in Western Massachusetts experienced the kind of incredible community and perhaps particular sense of ethnic identity that can occur in places that are somewhat "out of the way." However, and most importantly, I want to emphasize–for those of us who live in these places they are *not* out of the way; they are home. They are the center.

DAWN TASAKA STEFFLER is an Asian-American writer from Hawaii who currently lives in the San Francisco Bay Area. She was a *Smokelong Quarterly* Emerging Writer Fellow, winner of the Bath Flash Fiction Award, and selected for the *Wigleaf*

Top 50 long list. Her stories appear in places like *Pithead Chapel, Flash Frog, Fractured Lit, Moon City Review,* and *The Forge.* Find her online at dawntasakasteffler.com and on X, BlueSky and Instagram @dawnsteffler

In 2022, I was slogging through a novel. But I'm a magpie (aren't all writers magpies?) and something shiny caught my eye: an intriguing flash workshop called *A Smokelong Summer.* I knew nothing about flash and figured I could use a break from the novel. Famous last words because 1) I never returned to the novel, and 2) I have been exclusively writing flash ever since.

Our first assignment for *Smokelong Summer* was to make a list of ten possible topics to write about, and the seed for "How to Survive a Black Hole" was on that list. (A story about taking a trip to your hometown to move your parents into assisted living/memory care and then selling your childhood home, etc.) There are many real-life shards embedded in the story: memories of visiting my grandmother in a nursing home, a family member's problems with drug addiction, and

all the summers/winters I spent up in Tahoe with my husband and kids, some of them in wood-paneled rooms. But the story found its legs when the image of a fridge door embedded in drywall came to me. The bear motif was there from the very beginning, I think, because just a few months prior to me drafting the story, a bear broke into a friend's Tahoe cottage. Connecting the fridge door to a bear, to the funeral, to the overdose happened pretty rapid fire. The most fun part of revision was googling Hubble Telescope images and inserting something bear-ish into each section of the narrative. The most out-of-my-wheelhouse part of revision was digging deeper into my narrator's head (a math professor) and trying to see the world through a math and algorithms lens, as she probably would.

SARA J. STREETER (she/her), or 한혜숙 **HEA SOOK HAN**, is a writer and a Korean-American adoptee. She has been published in literary journals, such as *Cutleaf Journal, Longleaf Review, Hippocampus Magazine, Peatsmoke Journal, The Rappahan-*

nock Review, GASHER Journal, and others. Sara's creative nonfiction prose has been nominated for *Best of the Net, Best Microfiction,* and *Best Small Fictions.* Most recently, she was the Guest Editor for *Yellow Arrow Journal's* Vol. X, No. 1 (spring 2025). Sara lives in Silver Spring, Maryland, and works as an interior designer. Find her at sarajstreeter.com.

"The House Always Wins" is a fictionalized version of my life. When I started writing it in 2021, the brief time I spent in Toano, Virginia, was already distant, but the characters I met there, including the House, stuck with me. As an outsider (in more ways than one) to that environment, I was often uncomfortable and repulsed, and yet wildly mesmerized. It was an experience that shaped me in ways I'm still figuring out.

LISA WARTENBERG VÉLEZ is a Colombian writer of fiction who split her childhood between Bogota and South Florida. Her work has received creative and/or financial support from Bread Loaf Writers' Conference, Vermont Studio Center, Ucross Foundation, Kenyon Workshops, Tin House Workshops, and others. MFA: University of Houston (2023). Her work appears in *Michigan Quarterly Review, Cutleaf, Nimrod, Ghost Parachute,* and elsewhere, and is anthologized in *Best Debut Stories 2023* (Catapult) as a PEN / Dau Prize winner. She lives in Vermont.

I was facilitating an honors seminar for undergrads before I started writing this story. One particular student was writing a thesis centered on their data-oriented work in forensic anthropology at a South Texas facility, and their particular interest in the low representation of minorities in whole-body donation and high misidentification, especially of Latine and Asian people. That the most represented population in consensual cadaver donors are middle-class white men. This impacts how and whether criminal cases are resolved, as the anonymous victim's racial markers may be cross-referenced against shoddy data. I was struck by this. Through working with this student, I also learned how consensual donation is not the only source of whole-body donations. Some states allow the use of unidentified, unclaimed cadavers in anatomical education. It is the case in parts of Texas. I couldn't shake this. Couldn't shake the cold in those words. That the residue of class disparity could remain on the body postmortem haunted me.

From this emerged this story about a girl haunted by her father's disappearance as well as her own cruelty. It's also a story of how hard we are on those we love in spite of our highest intentions. How special it is to be held and loved, and to even have a human body, and how nothing can replace or erase the love given to us by our earliest caretakers. Through the story the girl awakens to her own queer longing, as she mourns the loss of her father.

South Florida was the partial backdrop of my youth, as was Colombia – both intense environments in which to become a person. I'm interested in the synergistic relationship between the wildness of that land, and the wildness of loving and losing someone, and how all of that can change someone. In this story, I also explore the profound loneliness of being odd and queer and alone in a land that seems built to eat you alive. And how it will eventually, anyways. And how sweet and urgent it is that we insist on making meaning of ourselves before it does.

As a Navy brat, **ROBERT YUNE** moved 11 times by the time he turned 18. After graduating from Pitt, he lived in Pittsburgh for the next 15 years. In the summer of 2012, he worked as a stand-in for George Takei and has appeared as an extra in commercials and movies such as *Me and Earl and the Dying Girl* and *Fathers and Daughters*. Yune's fiction has been published in *Green Mountains Review*, *The Kenyon Review*, and *Pleiades*, among others. In 2009, he received a writing fellowship from the Pennsylvania Council on the Arts. In 2015, his debut novel *Eighty Days of Sunlight* was nominated for the International Dublin Literary Award. His debut story collection *Impossible Children* won the 2017 Mary McCarthy Prize and was published by Sarabande Books.

"Princeton" was inspired by a true story my grandfather told me—it's reproduced nearly word-for-word in the piece. He actually owned a spirit bowl, which I once held in my hands. Later, when I was conducting research for this story, he mailed me a Polaroid of the bowl, which looked much different than the one I remember. I'm not sure what happened to it after he passed. Part of me wishes I'd tried harder to find it, and part of me is content to let it be, especially considering its history. Some things are best returned to the vast unknown.